D0631030

Lightning Strikes

Also From Lexi Blake

Masters And Mercenaries
The Dom Who Loved Me
The Men With The Golden Cuffs
A Dom Is Forever
On Her Master's Secret Service
Sanctum: A Masters and Mercenaries Novella
Love and Let Die
Unconditional: A Masters and Mercenaries Novella
Dungeon Royale
Dungeon Games: A Masters and Mercenaries Novella
A View to a Thrill
Cherished: A Masters and Mercenaries Novella
You Only Love Twice
Luscious: Masters and Mercenaries~Topped
Adored: A Masters and Mercenaries Novella
Master No
Just One Taste: Masters and Mercenaries~Topped 2
From Sanctum with Love
Devoted: A Masters and Mercenaries Novella
Dominance Never Dies
Submission is Not Enough, Coming October 25, 2016

Lawless
Ruthless
Satisfaction, Coming January 3, 2017

Masters Of Ménage (by Shayla Black and Lexi Blake)
Their Virgin Captive
Their Virgin's Secret
Their Virgin Concubine
Their Virgin Princess

Their Virgin Hostage
Their Virgin Secretary
Their Virgin Mistress

The Perfect Gentlemen (by Shayla Black and Lexi Blake
Scandal Never Sleeps
Seduction in Session
Big Easy Temptation

URBAN FANTASY

Thieves
Steal the Light
Steal the Day
Steal the Moon
Steal the Sun
Steal the Night
Ripper
Addict
Sleeper, Coming Soon

Lightning Strikes
By Lexi Blake

Rising Storm
Season 2
Episode 4

Story created by Julie Kenner and Dee Davis

EVIL EYE
CONCEPTS

Lightning Strikes, Episode 4
Rising Storm, Season 2
Copyright 2016 Julie Kenner and Dee Davis Oberwetter
ISBN: 978-1-942299-97-4

Published by Evil Eye Concepts, Incorporated

All rights reserved. No part of this book may be
reproduced, scanned, or distributed in any printed or
electronic form without permission. Please do not
participate in or encourage piracy of copyrighted materials
in violation of the author's rights.

This is a work of fiction. Names, places, characters, and
incidents are the product of the author's imagination and
are fictitious. Any resemblance to actual persons, living or
dead, events or establishments is solely coincidental.

Foreword

Dear reader –

We have wanted to do a project together for over a decade, but nothing really jelled until we started to toy with a kernel of an idea that sprouted way back in 2012 … and ultimately grew into Rising Storm.

We are both excited about and proud of this project—not only of the story itself, but also the incredible authors who have helped bring the world and characters we created to life.

We hope you enjoy visiting Storm, Texas. Settle in and stay a while!

Happy reading!

Julie Kenner & Dee Davis

Sign up for the Rising Storm/1001 Dark Nights Newsletter and be entered to win an exclusive lightning bolt necklace specially designed for Rising Storm by Janet Cadsawan of Cadsawan.com.

Go to www.RisingStormBooks.com to subscribe.

As a bonus, all subscribers will receive a free
Rising Storm story
Storm Season: Ginny & Jacob – the Prequel
by Dee Davis

Chapter One

Marcus Alvarez looked at the chaos on the kitchen table and wondered where his mother thought they were going to eat.

Joanne Alvarez rushed in, a harried smile on her face. "I'm sorry. I was up late last night folding those and I hadn't moved them yet. Give me a sec and I'll get this out of the way and we can set the table for breakfast."

He looked down at what had to be hundreds of pamphlets, all with Tate Johnson's smiling face on the front. The dark-haired man beamed out as though attempting to convince the world that all would be safe with him at the helm. *A Man You Can Trust.* That was the campaign slogan. He was running for mayor and Joanne was running his campaign.

Marcus quickly held a hand out, gesturing for his mother to stop. "I'll get it, Mom. You go back to making breakfast. Or better yet, why don't you grab some coffee and I'll make it for you."

His mother gave him a smile that actually went all the way to her eyes. "Don't be silly. I know Ian taught you a thing or two, but the kitchen is my domain. And thank you, sweetheart. If you could just box them up for me, I would appreciate it. I'm taking them all over town later today."

She was humming when she turned back into the kitchen.

Marcus sighed and started boxing up the pamphlets he was sure notified voters of how righteous and upstanding Tate Johnson was and how they would be fools to not want him as mayor.

He tried to think of what Sebastian Rush's campaign booklets would say. *A Man Who'll Get Your Daughters Pregnant* came to mind.

Yeah, he wasn't too happy with the senator. It didn't help that he knew for sure the senator and his indomitable mother wished Brittany would find another boyfriend. As he was her current boyfriend, he took offense.

He was happy his mother seemed to enjoy her new job, but he'd definitely had his fill of politicians.

"Let me help." His youngest sister took a stack of booklets and started packing them into the box set aside for them. "We were up late last night getting these suckers ready. I helped Mom with the design. Well, Luis and I did. He's pretty good with Photoshop."

His baby sister. It was so hard to figure out where the time had gone. He'd been away for so long and somehow Mallory had gone from a girl in pigtails to a young woman with a blossoming relationship and a confident smile.

Why had he stayed away from his family for so long?

Oh, yes. His rat bastard abusive father.

Marcus felt his mood lift in an instant. His father wasn't here and somehow that made the whole town a brighter place.

"Do you need a ride to school?" He packed the last of his mother's handiwork up and closed the box. The heavenly scent of bacon hit his nose.

Mallory shook her head. "Nope. It's a teacher in-service day. I'm free as a bird."

His mother's head poked out of the kitchen. "Free?"

Mallory's eyes widened as she realized her mistake. "I meant I'm totally free to go to the library and study really hard for my algebra test. So hard."

Marcus had to chuckle because his mother had been dragging them all into her never-ending quest to see Tate set up as the next mayor of Storm. In the last week, he'd helped clean out the back room at the new campaign headquarters that had apparently at one time served as a home to a family of raccoons. He'd been pressed into service evicting the little suckers. He'd hung campaign posters and taught his mom how to set up a mailing list.

Still, it was all worth it to see the energy she had now. His mother was lighter than before he'd left. He'd remembered a woman dulled by life. This Joanne Alvarez seemed to almost light up a room.

"That's such good news, honey." His mother winked at Mallory. "You can take a couple of stacks of those and put them on the circulation desk. I've already talked to the librarian. She's expecting them. Thank you. You're such a big help."

She turned and practically bounced back into the kitchen.

"Poor sister," he whispered. "Now you actually have to go to the library."

She grinned. "I'll make it a quick stop. You want some coffee?"

"Sure," he said. He glanced down at his cell and smiled at the text he'd received. His plans were going well.

"Can I have some?" Dakota stood in the doorway, still in her robe and slippers.

Dakota. His other sister. The one who'd gone from pigtails and asking for candy to ruining the lives of all around her by publicly outing the secrets of some of Storm's most powerful residents.

"Sure," Mallory said, giving her sister a slight smile.

Dakota moved to the table, slumping down in her chair. "Thanks."

Well, it was a start. There were days when getting any gratitude out of Dakota was like pulling teeth. "What are your plans for the day?"

Dakota sighed. "Well, I thought I'd watch some TV and then maybe do my nails. I have to do them myself now. Maybe later on I'll walk down the street and let people throw stuff at me."

He frowned. Despite what she'd done, she was still his sister. "Has someone done that to you?"

Her blue eyes turned up and a weary-looking smile hit her face. "Ready to take someone down for me, big brother?"

"Dakota, if someone's physically assaulted you, then yes. I'm going to need a name." He knew a lot of people were angry with her for what she'd done at the picnic. He'd hoped with a little time they would forgive and forget, but he feared the Rushes kept stoking the fire against his sister.

His sister was out of a job and couldn't find a place to live, but Senator Rush had just been reelected. By the skin of his teeth, but the nasty bastard still had his job even after he'd been caught sleeping with not one but two of the town's young women. Ginny Moreno was very likely carrying the man's child. But it was Dakota who was being punished the worst in his mind. Yes, she'd been involved with the senator, too, and that had been wrong. Yes, she'd been the one to out the situation in the worst possible way, but he wasn't about to allow anyone to abuse her.

Dakota held a hand up. "Thanks for the save, Sir Marcus, but my stoning is more figurative than literal. No one's physically hurting me, but it's still hard to walk into a room and have the whole place go silent. I know the minute I step outside everyone stares and talks behind their hands.

It's why I think I'm going to be a shut-in. I can live here for the rest of my miserable life. I'll be that weird old lady who never goes outside. Maybe I should get a cat. Or twelve."

Mallory stepped back out and put a mug in front of Dakota. "Or you could try being nice to people."

Dakota's eyes rolled. "Like that works. Thanks."

Mallory's shoulders shrugged. "You're welcome. But seriously, you have to get out there. You've been hiding in this house and it just makes it worse when you do go out."

His mother stepped out of the kitchen, a stack of plates in her hand. "Mallory's right."

Dakota stared at her mother sullenly. "You always think Mallory's right."

"Of course I don't," his mother replied patiently. "But in this case, she is. You have to get out and act like nothing's wrong. Eventually people will get on board. If you don't give them anything else to talk about, time will do the job of putting distance between you and the incident."

His mother knew how to do that. She smiled even when it hurt. She ignored the bruises on her body and the ache in her soul, and everyone eventually treated it like it was her normal state.

Yeah, that was why he'd left.

"It's easy for you to say," Dakota replied, but she stood up and took the plates from her mother's hand and started to set the table.

It was a true turnaround for her. Somehow the weeks of being stuck in the house and forced to look inward had brought about small but good changes in Dakota. It was precisely why he was willing to do what he was about to do.

"What if I told you I got you a job interview?" Marcus asked.

Dakota stopped, her hand still on a plate. "Where? Is it like janitorial? Because I'm not cleaning toilets. I don't care. I'd rather be a cat lady."

"Then you have to clean out litter boxes," Mallory said with a grin.

"Fine. I'll collect animals who don't poop. That'll be my thing." Dakota set the plate down and faced him. "Do you seriously think you can get me a job interview? Because I've tried everywhere. No one will even talk to me."

He'd already taken care of that. "You've got an interview this morning at Pink. Ten o'clock."

Her eyes lit up. "The clothing store? The one on the square?"

At least he was making someone happy this morning. "That one. Courtney Kline owns the shop and her father used to be my Boy Scout troop leader and he coached the Little League. She's a nice lady and she's willing to give you a shot. But you should probably shower."

Her normally lengthy beauty routine had been tossed aside in favor of staying in her robe almost all day.

"I'll be ready." There was suddenly a bounce to Dakota's step that had been missing for weeks. "No time for breakfast, Mom."

"You could have toast." His mother sighed as Dakota strode back toward her bedroom. "I'll take her some in a bit. That was a very nice thing you did for your sister."

"We do what we have to." He was the man of the house now, and it didn't feel as constricting as he'd thought it would. It was a revelation. He thought he'd be desperate to get back to Montana by now, but he'd settled back in. Without his father around, the bonds of responsibility didn't chafe the way they used to.

And then there was Brittany.

She needed him, too. No matter what her family thought.

There was a knock on the door. Mallory ran off to see who was there.

"Well, you should know I'm very proud of the way

you're handling yourself, son." His mother reached out and squeezed his arm. "I've been so happy to have you around to lean on."

"You haven't been leaning much, Mom. I don't know if you've noticed but you're kind of bossy lately," he teased.

She flushed and her hand went to her cheek. "I'm certainly not, Marcus. I'm simply doing my job."

"Good morning, Joanne," a deep voice said.

His mother flushed a deeper pink as she turned and saw Sheriff Dillon Murphy standing in the room. He had his hat in hand and nodded their way.

"Apparently he was patrolling the neighborhood, looking for bacon," Mallory quipped.

It was the sheriff's turn to flush. "I was close by and I thought I would check up on you. But if you do have extra, I haven't eaten."

"Of course, that would be lovely. We're just about ready." She hurried back into the kitchen.

"Do you mind?" Dillon asked.

"Of course not." Marcus nodded Dillon's way. The sheriff was practically family. Marcus always felt at home when he was with the Murphys. He wanted Dillon to feel the same.

The fact that he was pretty sure his mother was falling for the sheriff probably should have bothered him, but Dillon was the one who made her smile, encouraged her to be independent. From what he could tell, the blooming friendship with Dillon was good for his mom.

"But don't think you're eating all the bacon," he warned.

Dillon gave him a brilliant smile and sat down across from where his mom would sit. In the chair that used to be Hector's.

That didn't bother Marcus at all. That was a damn fine sight.

Marcus sat down, ready to face the day. It looked like it would be a good one.

* * * *

Dakota looked at herself in the mirror and acknowledged that she was nervous. She hated being nervous.

Her makeup was flawless, her hair proper and professional. Well, as professional as she needed to be. It was too pretty to put in some fussy old-lady bun. She couldn't help it she had naturally sexy hair.

It didn't make her a slut, though some people seemed to think it did.

Or maybe it was the fact that she'd slept with someone else's husband.

Damn it. She didn't like thinking about it. It hadn't been her fault. Except weeks of thinking about it made her wonder if it wasn't really. Maybe she could have handled things better than she had.

Was that lipstick right? Should she go with something a little pinker?

After all, the store was called Pink. This Courtney person must like pink.

"You want to borrow my sweater? The one I got at Pink?" Mallory asked, leaning against the doorjamb.

"You shop there?"

Mallory shrugged. "Mostly I window shop, but I bought that sweater with my birthday money. They've got cute clothes. You would like them. I think it would be a perfect job for you."

She glanced over at her sister. Somehow she felt closer to her after the debacle on Founders' Day. Mallory had been pretty cool. She'd come and dragged her out of her room a couple of nights back and forced her to sit and watch some dumb rom com with their mom. It had been a silly film, but she'd laughed and actually eaten some of the popcorn her mom had made.

It had been nice.

"Thanks," she said. "It might be lucky for me to wear something from the store."

"I'll go get it. It'll look perfect with your white skirt."

Dakota nodded and turned back to the mirror. She missed her father. Still. Even after all these months, she missed him, but she was oddly starting to like her mom. Turns out she wasn't so bad when she was on her own. Dakota didn't like the way the sheriff kept sniffing around, but it wasn't like her mom would ever return the jerk's affection or anything.

Focus. She had to focus on getting this job and getting back on her feet.

"I made you one of those smoothie things you used to love. It's banana with some fresh peach and a scoop of the protein powder Marcus uses. You can't walk into that interview with your hands shaking." Her mother stood in the hallway, a travel mug in her hand.

It was the kind of thing that usually bugged her. She didn't need her mom up in her business. Still, she reached for the smoothie. Somehow having the whole world hate her had made her see her mom in a bit of a different light. Joanne really had kept things together after Daddy left. Maybe it was time to cut her some slack. "Thanks. I can use it. I'm a little nervous."

Her mom's head shook. "Not my Dakota. You've got nothing to be nervous about. You hold your head high and walk into that interview with pride. You did a good job at the bank."

For the most part. She'd certainly been way more fun to work with than the old biddies who ran the place. "I was good."

"The only reason you lost that job was Marylee Rush."

The bitch. It didn't seem to matter to her that her own son was a complete pervert. Marylee Rush was a "shoot the messenger" kind of woman. Shoot her. Kick her out of her apartment. Make sure no one else would hire her. "What if she talks to Courtney Kline? What if this is completely useless and I'm just fooling myself?"

"You can do anything you set your mind to, Dakota. Maybe you get this job, maybe you don't, but you can't give up. You have to keep trying and something good will come along."

She wished she could believe that. "Do you think Tate's going to win the election next spring? If he does, are you going to work for the mayor's office?"

It was a question she would have found completely ridiculous a year ago. A year ago her mother spent all her time on the house and still didn't manage to get much done. Now she seemed so much more competent than she used to be. She even seemed to have found a way to be more graceful. Her mother was one of the clumsiest human beings on the planet, but lately she'd seemed to turn it around. She hadn't fallen or walked into a door in the longest time.

It wasn't so crazy to think she might be able to work for the mayor.

"I don't know," she said softly, a wistful look on her face. "I hope so. I think Tate is an excellent candidate and he's got a good shot. If he wants me to help him out after the election, I would definitely think about it."

"You like working." It was a revelation. She'd always kind of thought of her mother as lazy. Her dad complained about it. She hadn't looked lazy last night when she'd been folding her little booklet things. She'd looked energetic and alive.

"I do. I really like it, Dakota."

"You like it more than you liked being a housewife. I

know you worked at the flower shop, but that was part time. This is more serious and you seem to really like it more than you did being home most of the time." She hadn't meant for it to sound like an accusation. She really hadn't.

Her mom's face softened. "I love being a mom to you and Mallory and Marcus. You three kids were my whole world most of my life. But you don't need me the way you used to. I like being needed. I like having something to do. It's why you're so miserable right now. You need something in your life. A job or a passion or maybe even school. Have you thought about it? I'm making a little money. I could afford some classes if you want to go back."

She'd actively hated college. "Not for a second. I've had all the school I need. But you're right. I do need to do something. I need to be out there showing all those hypocrites that they can't break me."

"Just go in with a positive attitude."

"It's hard to have that lately. It seems like everyone caught in the scandal's been forgiven except me." It wasn't fair. It wasn't right. She'd been the innocent one.

"I don't think Ginny Moreno feels very forgiven," her mother pointed out.

At least Ginny would likely get a decent monetary settlement out of it. The Rush family would either pay her child support or a ton of money to keep her mouth shut. Dakota hadn't gotten a dime. She'd gotten scorn. "Well, at least I didn't get pregnant. I guess I should be thankful for small blessings."

Her mother stared at her for a moment. "Why do you hate that girl?"

She didn't like the look on her mom's face. It cut through her. How could she make her understand? "I cared about Jacob. A lot. I suppose you could say I didn't like the idea of Ginny using him the way she did. I miss him."

He was supposed to have been her ticket out of this town. Jacob was supposed to love her back.

Why did the men she love always leave her?

Her mother reached out and smoothed back her hair, a gesture Dakota hadn't allowed in a very long time. It felt good now. "I'm sorry about Jacob, but you have to move on. It's time for you to look to your future. Marcus has set this up for you. All you have to do is smile and show that woman how powerful you are. You know if you ever decided to do something really good with your life, you would be amazing."

She wasn't concerned about good. But if her brother could help her get a job and get back on her feet, she would take it as a win. Dakota took a sip of the shake. It wasn't half bad. On impulse, she leaned over and kissed her mom's cheek. "Thanks."

"You're welcome," her mom replied, surprise obvious in her tone. "Go get dressed. I'm going to head out with the sheriff. He's helping me move some furniture into the campaign headquarters."

Yeah, Dakota just bet he was. Dillon Murphy was trying to get into her mom's granny panties, but Dakota was sure it wouldn't work. Her mom was way too boring to ever have an affair. If she used the sheriff for physical labor, who was Dakota to say no? It made her think her mom was way smarter than she'd given her credit for. "Okay, wish me luck."

"Good luck, baby girl."

Dakota joined Mallory and got ready to start the next phase of her life.

* * * *

Hector Alvarez sat in his car watching the house he'd bought, the one he'd provided for his family. He'd been the king of that castle until the damn sheriff had decided to come in and take what belonged to Hector.

He could still feel the humiliation burning in him, still see that bastard standing over him and telling him to get out of town or he would tell the town what he'd seen.

What had Dillon Murphy seen? He'd seen Hector dealing with his wife. Joanne was his. His. He had the right to deal with her any way he saw fit. He was the one who had put up with her for years, dealt with her lazy ways. Joanne required a firm hand.

The door to the house opened and he saw a man walk out.

Marcus. Marcus had come home. His only son had walked out, leaving his family for some ranch in Montana. Hector had thought it was a stupid fit at the time, a rebellion, but then Marcus had stayed away.

Now he was back and his son looked like a man. Marcus held the door open and smiled down at the girl who walked through.

Mallory. His youngest. Such a pretty girl, but far too influenced by her mother. She wouldn't amount to anything because Joanne had ruined her. It seemed like it was his wife's goal in life to make their children as weak as she was.

Mallory strode off, a bag over her shoulder. She walked down the street with a smile on her face. Like nothing was wrong with the world. Like she was happy.

Like she didn't miss her father at all.

Marcus moved to his car, opening the door for his other sister.

Dakota. His baby girl. Now there was a daughter. He stared at her. Of all the things he'd done, leaving Dakota actually made him feel a little guilty. She was the only one who took after him, the only of his children to truly see him as he was. Dakota understood.

She slipped in the car and then Marcus took off.

It was not lost on Hector that the sheriff's squad car was sitting in front of his house.

Was Dillon Murphy inside trying to take his place? Trying to get his wife in bed?

Rage threatened to take over, the emotion rolling in his gut.

Was he putting his hands all over Joanne? Hector tightened his grip on the steering wheel and he fought the urge to stalk in and wrap his own hands around the sheriff's throat.

And then he would deal with his wife.

The door opened and the man in question stepped out, carrying a box. Joanne followed, turning and locking the door behind her.

Had she changed the locks on him? She would find out there wasn't a lock made that would keep him out of his own home. He was done playing the victim.

Joanne was wearing a skirt and a blouse that showed off far too much of her cleavage. When had she started dressing like a whore? Likely around the time she'd taken the sheriff into her bed.

Joanne followed behind Murphy like a puppy after its master. She was smiling and laughed at one point as they got into the cruiser and drove away like it was their right to be together.

Hector sat in the seat of his car and stared out. She'd walked away from him. She'd smiled and gone on with her life like he didn't matter.

He was her husband and she was welcoming another man into his home.

It was past time to take his rightful place back. It was time to show his wife, the sheriff, and the whole town who he really was.

Storm was going to find out that Hector Alvarez was back to stay.

Chapter Two

Joanne Alvarez liked riding in a police cruiser. Of course she was in the front of the vehicle and not the back. She was sure that made a difference.

"You comfortable?" Dillon stopped at the stoplight in the center of town. He was staring forward, his square jaw on display.

He was the most beautiful man she'd ever seen.

"Absolutely. You have a very luxurious way to haul prisoners around," she said with a smile on her face. There was a little piece of her that was disappointed though. They'd been alone for a few moments inside the house. Marcus had gone off to call on Brittany and the girls had been getting dressed. It had just been her and Dillon.

They'd stood in the living room and stared at each other for a moment, the kiss they'd shared sitting between them like a landmine waiting to go off. In a good way. She had to admit, they had chemistry.

Unfortunately, it wasn't enough.

She hadn't been able to reach out to him. She wanted to. She'd wanted to step into his strong arms and feel them close around her as his mouth moved over hers. She'd never felt more like a woman than the minute Dillon Murphy had kissed her. Her body had gone soft and she'd thought that maybe this time she would find out why women read romance novels and chased after men. She wanted to know why she got so breathless around him and if there was anything at the end of that particular road. But she couldn't.

She was married. She'd made commitments and she had to honor them.

It was why she kept to her side of the car now.

"Yeah, we don't consider this luxurious," Dillion said with a grimace. "These cars are ten years old."

She shrugged. "When you drive what I drive, anything that runs with regularity feels like a luxury car."

Hector had taken the only good vehicle. He'd left her with nothing. No money. No decent transportation. No way to make the mortgage. Those first few weeks when she'd realized he wasn't coming back had been rough. She'd had no skills, no confidence in herself.

Somehow she'd pulled through, and that had a lot to do with the man at her side.

"Well maybe next spring, once the election is over, you can talk to the mayor," she offered.

He nodded her way. "Absolutely. Zeke is a tightwad with the budget. We had to set up a speed trap just to get a new coffeemaker. Do you have any idea what cops are like when they're not properly caffeinated?"

The man could make her smile like no one else. "I'm sure it's a real problem. If Tate's elected, I'll definitely talk to him about the mayor's office looking into the issue."

The light changed and Dillon turned right, moving toward the campaign office. They had a delivery of furniture today that she couldn't miss. This would be their work home until the election, and she needed to make it perfect for the people who would be working for them. They would mostly be volunteers and she owed them a nice place to work.

Tate had taken a real chance on her, and she didn't mean to let him down. This job was the best thing that had happened to her in a long time.

The kiss whispered across her brain again. Dillon's lips on hers, brushing lightly. Her skin had lit up, her whole body flaring to life. Nothing in her life had been as erotic as that one kiss.

She didn't want the morning to end. It had been so nice sitting and having breakfast as a family. And, yes, part of that had been Dillon sitting across from her, making jokes with Marcus and asking Mallory about how school was going.

The minute they got to the campaign office, she would have to be professional, keep herself apart from him. They would have eyes on them, people watching their every move. It wouldn't do to have Tate's campaign manager gossiped about. The lord knew her family had enough gossip about them. Given the fact that her own sister, Hannah, had dated Tate and then slept with his brother, Tucker, Joanne counted herself lucky to have the job she did. She wasn't about to risk it.

Not when she had nothing to give Dillon.

What would she do if Hector wasn't standing in the way? If she was free and she didn't have to worry about her marriage?

Would she be bold and brave and kiss him? Would she stop him right here in the square and turn to him, tilting her face up, and demand that he kiss her again?

She didn't have that right. Worse than that, she didn't have any rights where Dillon was concerned. Eventually he would have to run for his office again. He couldn't have an affair with a married woman. Not that she would do that. Except she thought about it a lot. If people seriously suspected that they were flirting, the gossip would start and that could hurt Dillon's campaign. Would she be the thing that dragged him down?

Or the one that lifted him up?

She turned, her line of thought a bit too much to take this early in the morning. A familiar figure walked down the sidewalk, heading toward Cuppa Joe's. He was an attractive man wearing jeans and a Western shirt. The boots on his feet were worn from use and the hat on his head was a Stetson. Ian Briggs was a real cowboy. "Is that Ian?"

"I do believe it is." Dillon pulled up to the curb, pressing the button that brought the window down. "Hey there, Ian. How are you this morning?"

Ian was the man who'd taken her son in when he'd gone off to the wilds of Montana. She was fairly certain Ian was responsible for the amazing man her son was becoming. She definitely knew it hadn't been her husband's influence.

Marcus had left her house a rebellious child and returned a confident man, willing to accept the challenge of taking care of his family and his girlfriend. She was so proud of him.

Ian leaned over and gave them both a big smile. "I'm just getting started. Thought I'd head in and grab some coffee to start the morning right. It's a beautiful day, isn't it?"

"Did Anna Mae forget to bring you coffee with your breakfast?" Joanne asked. Ian was staying at the Flower Hill B&B. Anna Mae and Rita Mae were famous for taking care of their guests' needs, and breakfast there always came with unlimited coffee.

Dillon chuckled beside her. "I think he prefers the coffee here."

Ian nodded. "There is something special about it."

He was awfully cheerful, but then the rumor was the

Montana rancher was sweet on Marisol Moreno, who happened to own and run Cuppa Joe's. Apparently since Ian had hit town looking for Marcus, he'd become one of the coffeehouse's biggest customers.

"It certainly is," Dillon replied. "How's the ranch hunt going?"

She was so happy Ian had decided to move part of his cattle ranch business down here to Storm. It meant Marcus would have an easier time staying close to home. And that he would have a wonderful male role model around. "Yes, have you had any luck?"

He shrugged, an easy roll of his shoulders. "I'll work it all out. I have to say I'm happy here. It's a nice little town you have. I'm looking forward to visiting often."

"Well, if you find yourself in need of some home cooking, you feel free to come by any night." She owed the man for watching out for her boy.

"Except Friday," Dillon corrected, proving he knew her schedule better than she did. "There's a fund raiser for Tate Johnson's mayoral campaign then. She's kind of running that sucker."

Ian nodded. "I heard about that. I think I'll have to come to that and see what Mr. Johnson has to say. After all, in a way, this is going to be my town, what with Marcus running a ranch for me down here. I should get to know everyone. You two have a nice day. Mrs. Alvarez, I'll see you later. I'm coming by this afternoon to talk to Marcus about how we're going to move the cattle. I hope you don't mind us using your dining room to talk."

Her boy was a ranch hand, but she wouldn't be at all surprised if one day he owned his own ranch. Ian was teaching him everything he needed to know. He was being the father Marcus had always deserved.

"Not at all. I'll look forward to it." She genuinely would. She loved how her house was now a hub for socialization. Mallory's friends dropped by all the time. Brittany Rush would show up to visit with Marcus. The sweet girl was always willing to lend a hand to whatever Joanne was doing. Dakota didn't have friends, but it was nice sometimes to have her home.

Her house seemed so full of life now. Once it had seemed like a prison, but now it was filled with light and laughter. She loved going home at the end of a long day. It had become her sanctuary.

Guilt swamped her. She'd made promises to her husband, but she was happier with him gone. What kind of woman did that make her? She was struggling to reconcile the Joanne she'd been before with the woman who had emerged with Hector gone.

Dillon wished Ian well and started moving again. "He's going to overdose on caffeine before Marisol gives in and goes on a date with him. It's good to know there's some competition for that lady. Maybe this is the kick in the pants Patrick needs to finally make a move and get his girl."

He maneuvered his way to the back of the building that housed the campaign offices. It had become her little home away from home. She was in charge in that building.

"I've got the rest of the day off. Let's see if we can whip this place into shape," Dillon said, pulling into a parking space. "And remember this when you're a high-powered politico and thinking about the budget for the lowly sheriff's office. We really need one of those coffeemakers with the cup things."

She felt a smile slide over her face. "I'll see what I can do about it."

But when she got out of the car, a chill crawled over her skin. She stopped and looked around. It was quiet at this time of day. Cuppa Joe's was busy and the Bluebonnet Cafe had its share of customers, but the rest of the square was quiet.

So why did she feel eyes on her? Someone was watching her. She could feel it along her skin, down to her bones.

Dillon walked around the car, standing next to her. "Hey, are you all right?"

He seemed to be able to sense her moods in a way no one else ever had—or had never taken the time to. Joanne looked around, trying to figure out where the anxiety was coming from. Nothing. She saw absolutely nothing out of the ordinary. The sky above was a pure blue, the air around her sweet. It was a perfect day.

She was being silly.

"I'm wonderful. Let's get started."

* * * *

Ian Briggs strode into Cuppa Joe's, putting his best "I'm perfectly harmless, you shouldn't be afraid of me" smile on his face. It was the one he used for Marisol Moreno. It was the one meant to ease her into being comfortable around him. Like a deer he was trying to feed from his hand.

Or a woman he really wanted to get into his arms.

He stared at her for a moment, taking his place at the back of the line. This was her natural habitat. She had on jeans and a blouse that was covered by her crisp white apron. Her hair was pulled back, revealing the graceful line of her neck and delicate jaw. Her eyes were big and dark and they sparkled as she smiled at her customers, sliding a mug of coffee their way.

He had it bad for that woman and damn if that didn't feel good.

So long. He'd spent forever in a kind of purgatory. He might have walked out of prison, but that had just been his body. His soul had stayed there for the longest time. He'd spent years awash in guilt and mourning and rage.

He knew everyone thought he was so good to Marcus, that he was Marcus's savior. How could he explain that Marcus was the one who'd saved him?

"I swear it was him," the woman in front of him whispered to her friend.

"How could you tell? Did you talk to him?" the other woman asked, her voice low.

"I saw him through the window of his car. He was just driving around like nothing was wrong," she continued.

Ian ignored the gossip. He'd gotten a decent working knowledge of Storm since he'd come here, but he knew small towns thrived on gossip, none of it good.

He wished he could fix Marcus's problems with gossip. The Rushes were still coming at him hard and it was going to kill that boy if he lost Brittany over her family's bigotry.

He moved up as the line moved, watching how Marisol handled her customers. If thinking about the Rushes made him see red, watching her brought him peace.

"Hey, Ian. You here for the coffee or the scenery?" a familiar voice asked from behind.

He hated the fact that he could still blush like a damn schoolgirl. He turned and put his hand out, greeting the man he thought of as his son. "Marcus, you know I'm hell on wheels without my coffee."

Marcus grinned, shaking his hand. "I also know that you could have had a cup at the B&B."

"I like this coffee better."

A smirk hit Marcus's face. He loved that the kid smiled so readily now. In the beginning, he'd done nothing but bark and growl at everyone around him. "It's the same beans. Marisol supplies the B&B."

Damn it. Did the kid have to be such a smart ass? "Well, there must be something special about the way they brew it then."

Marcus bit back a laugh. "Okay. If that's the way you're

going to play it."

"What's got you in such a good mood?"

"I got Dakota a job interview," Marcus revealed, satisfaction plain on his face. "As long as she doesn't screw it up, she should be working at Pink in a few days, and that means my plan is starting to roll out."

"You have a plan? I've never known you to have a plan." He could play the sarcasm game, too.

"If I can get Dakota out of the house and back on her feet, there's a lot of pressure off my mom. With Dakota gone, she'll only have to take care of Mallory and the house, and she's actually making decent money for the first time in her life."

Marcus's plan became very clear. "Ah, you think Dakota moving out clears the way for you to get your own place."

Marcus nodded. "Bingo. It's not that I don't love my family."

"But you're a man and you need your space," Ian finished. "As soon as we get the ranch up and running, you know you're going to have to live there."

"Naturally." Marcus moved with him as the line got closer to the front. "I've already thought about how I want to build the ranch house."

It was good to know the boy was thinking. "Build?"

Marcus held up his hands. "These two hands can do amazing things. I know it sounds crazy, but I think it would be kind of cool to build it myself. Kind of like starting something important."

Ian felt his heart seize with emotion. Marcus was talking about starting his future, something he would pass down to his children. He was talking about a legacy.

Though they didn't share an ounce of blood, somehow this boy had become his son. So many years spent thinking the universe was unkind. Sometimes the universe simply needed time to balance the scales again. He would never stop missing his son, but he was grateful for the chance at another family. He wasn't going to screw it up this time. "I think that sounds like a perfect plan, son."

He would help him. They would build a new homestead down here in Texas for Marcus. He would go back to Montana, satisfied that Marcus was well set up.

Could he be satisfied back in Montana when the only woman to stir his blood in years was here in Texas?

"All I need is Dakota to go in and act like a real live human being for once in her life." Marcus frowned as though he realized how low the likelihood of that prospect was. "Maybe I should go back and sit with her."

"She has to stand on her own two feet sometime."

"Yeah, sometimes I think her feet are actually cloven hooves," Marcus admitted. "But she has been better lately."

He would hate to have seen her when she wasn't better. That girl had an attitude on her and it wasn't a pleasant one. "Do you think it will be easier to see Brittany if you move out?"

"I know it will." Marcus sighed. "Right now, I'm not welcome at her place and she can't feel comfortable at mine. Not with Dakota there."

He'd heard the story. "I can't imagine she'll ever be comfortable around your sister. I like Brittany. She's a sweetheart, but it seems to me the two of you are quickly becoming this town's Romeo and Juliet. I don't want to see that happen."

Marcus stared up at the menu Ian was fairly certain he had memorized. "I don't know about that, but I do know we can't find out if we'll work if the pressure never comes off us. I think about it a lot. I think about whether or not she can ever really be happy with someone like me."

"Someone like you?"

"A working man," he said with grim resolve. "I'm

going to be a rancher and that means hard work, and everything we make will go back into the ranch for a while. It's not an easy life, but it's the one I want. I don't know that I would be good at anything else."

For the first time since he'd come up with his plan, Ian felt a moment of doubt. Was he putting Marcus in a corner? Was there something else out there he wanted to do? "You know if you want to go back to school or get training for some other job, I would help you do that. You don't have to be stuck on a ranch the rest of your life."

"Stuck?" Marcus looked at him like he'd grown two heads. "I'm not stuck on the ranch. I love it. It's the only place I really feel comfortable. That's what I'm saying. I'm never going to fit into her world."

Something eased inside Ian's chest. "I'm glad to hear it. There's nothing else like it. I'm most comfortable when I'm working, too. But I think you might be underestimating that girl. She might have been born with a silver spoon in her mouth, but she's got a backbone. She'll make up her own mind and then you'll know she's with you because she loves you and not for any other reason."

He said the words, but he meant them, too. Not just for Marcus. Maybe he was starting to mean them for himself.

"Hey, I just got a text from Dakota that the interview is over and she's heading to the campaign office. I should probably head her off at the pass. I think Dillon's still with Mom, so I want to referee that meeting. I'm going to pass on the coffee." Marcus was looking down at his cell phone.

"I'll bring you some," Ian offered. "I know what you like. You go on and deal with your family. I was hoping we could go over some plans I have for the ranch this afternoon. If we're getting into organic ranching, we have to change some of our practices."

Marcus stepped out of line. "You're a lifesaver. And

thank you. Keep your fingers crossed that Dakota got the job. See you in a bit."

Ian turned and stepped up to the counter.

Marisol stopped and stared for the barest moment before her professional smile came back on her face. "What can I do for you today, Mr. Briggs?"

So polite. If she knew what he really wanted her to do for him, she would likely run the other way. Or maybe not. He could feel the chemistry between them. Surely she could, too. Still, he had to take it slow with her. "I would love two large coffees, one perfectly preserved and the other with so much sugar in it you could count it as a dessert."

Her lips curled up in genuine mirth. "Ah, you're ordering for Marcus. I always ask him if he wants coffee with his cream and sugar. But you're a purist, aren't you?"

"That is not to say I don't like things sweet from time to time, but your coffee needs absolutely nothing to make it perfect. It's already there."

And there it was, that little beat of breathiness, that slight widening of her eyes that let him know she wasn't immune to him. If he was patient, he could move her toward the possibility of seeing him outside the coffee shop.

She straightened and that professional look was back on her face. "That's kind of you to say, Mr. Briggs. I'll go and get your order."

She turned and he was treated to her very feminine, curvy backside. That was one woman who looked good from every angle. Oddly it wasn't her beauty that caused him to have such a strong connection with her. Marisol Moreno exuded a quiet strength that called to him. It was like a siren song he couldn't quite resist.

He watched as she walked to the other side of the counter, moving gracefully as she poured the coffee. She stopped and leaned over, saying something to the two women who'd been in front of him. They leaned in, one with a gleam in her eyes. Yep. He knew that look. She had some good gossip and couldn't wait to tell it. She spoke to Marisol, whose spine straightened suddenly.

She turned back to Ian. "Where did Marcus go?"

"He went to Tate Johnson's campaign office," Ian replied. "He's meeting Dakota there. What's wrong?"

There was fear in Marisol's eyes.

"The rumor is Hector Alvarez was seen driving around town earlier this morning," she said in a whisper. "I don't know how much you know about Marcus's father, but that could be very bad for Joanne."

He knew enough. "I'll have to take a rain check."

She nodded. "Be safe."

He turned and strode out of the shop. He needed to warn Marcus.

This time if Hector Alvarez thought he could abuse his son, he was going to have to go through Ian.

Chapter Three

Joanne stepped back and looked at her handiwork. Well, Dillon's handiwork. It helped to have a ridiculously tall man around.

"It's weird seeing my face everywhere." Tate frowned as he looked up at the massive poster Dillon had just finished hanging.

"Yeah," Dillon chimed in. "Are you wearing makeup in that shot?"

She turned to Tate. "It's working quite well with the focus groups. We sent this set of campaign shots and the new slogans and they tested incredibly high. And you look very masculine."

Tate stared up at the poster as though he wasn't convinced. "I don't know that I'm in love with the idea of focus groups. I worry about what the people of Storm are going to think."

The door opened and she noticed Dakota walking in. It was good to see her up and out of bed. And dressed appropriately for once. Maybe working at Pink would force her out of the Daisy Dukes and crop tops she seemed to think were proper business attire. Dakota stopped and looked up at the wall mural.

"Huh, you actually look pretty hot. I didn't think that was possible," she said with a shake of her head.

Tate nodded. "All right then. We'll go with this one."

Dillon chuckled. "Well, we know where your priorities are."

"Hey, Dakota's nothing if not honest when it comes to stuff like this," Tate replied.

"Yeah, those last shots made you look fat." Dakota sat on one of the desks like she owned the place. Her daughter was good at that.

"Dakota, that was rude." She felt her cheeks flame.

"Well, they did." Dakota showed not an ounce of remorse. "And that brown they put him in completely washed out his skin tone. This one's good. He should wear darker colors and the tie brings out his eyes. It's got a good vibe. It says 'I'm probably not going to sleep with a bunch of young girls and potentially get them pregnant.'"

"Dakota!" Why did her daughter have the most bent sense of humor?

Tate chuckled. "I'm very glad it's got a good vibe. Everything is falling into place, Joanne. And the office is shaping up. How many staffers do we have?"

She was so happy to talk about something that didn't remind the world of Dakota's issues. "Three, but we'll bring in more volunteers as we get closer to the election. I've got everything set up. And I have your office in the back."

"She made me move the furniture around," Dillon interjected. "Apparently the mayor's office is already using the sheriff's department to do the heavy lifting."

Everyone seemed to need to tease her today, but she couldn't help but smile at Dillon. He'd been an amazing sport. He'd taken her direction and encouraged her to make all the decisions.

They made a good team.

Maybe she should think about asking him to come to dinner. Nothing big at first. Just two friends. They could see how the town handled it. It could be like their own focus group.

"Come on back." Dillon nodded Tate's way. "I don't think the desk is where you're going to want it, but it's a heavy sucker. Can you give me a hand? It's too big for Joanne to help."

"Sure thing. Let's take a look." He walked back, talking to Dillon and thanking him for all the help.

"Thanks for being kind to Tate about his picture." She was going to look on the bright side. Tate had been on the fence about the picture and now he felt good about it. She was going to hang on to that.

Dakota shrugged. "He does look good. I try to never lie about stuff like that."

"How did the interview go?"

"Okay, I guess. I don't know. Women don't tend to like me. I think it's because they're jealous. But I answered all her questions and stuff."

Women didn't like Dakota because they could tell how difficult she would be, but Joanne wasn't about to start a war. "I'll keep my fingers crossed for you."

There was a long pause and Joanne went back to straightening out her desk.

"Do you think they'll ever forgive me, Mama?"

She glanced up and Dakota looked more vulnerable than Joanne could remember in years. She moved to Dakota, reaching out to her. "Oh, baby, they'll forget. I promise you. This is going to blow over."

For the first time in forever, Dakota leaned on her. "I hate having to beg. I just wish things were like they were before. I never thought I would say that. I thought I hated that job, but I hate this more."

"You need to give it time and you need to show a little

humility."

Dakota groaned. "I hate that word. I don't even really know what it means."

That was so apparent. "It just means be nicer to the people around you. Maybe you think about finding the things you like about people and complimenting them on that instead of pointing out their flaws. I know you think you're helping them, but it hurts people's feelings."

"I'm just being honest." The words were sullen, but Dakota laid her head on Joanne's shoulder.

"Try to be a little less honest about how fat you think people are." It felt good to stroke her daughter's hair. It reminded her that once Dakota had been a little girl who smiled and tried to please the people around her.

Then Hector had ruined her. He'd allowed Dakota to do whatever she liked without any repercussions. She'd always known the world would catch up to her baby girl, but just not how jarring the crash would be.

"I guess I could be a little nicer. I tried to be nice to Courtney Kline. I didn't mention that the jeans she was wearing were mom jeans and they didn't flatter her figure."

"What's wrong with mom jeans?"

Dakota brought her head back up and a little smile lit her face. "No one should wear them. They're for the elderly."

Joanne frowned. "I wear mom jeans."

"See, I told you for the elderly." But there was a smile on Dakota's face, a genuine one.

"I am not elderly." Not at all. She would admit that sometimes she felt old, but lately she was finding her youth again. "Maybe I should get new jeans. What do they call them? Skinny jeans?"

Dakota laughed. "Absolutely. We should get you some skinny jeans with bling on the butt."

She had to draw the line somewhere. "I am not putting

diamonds on my derriere."

"What?" Marcus walked into the room, his eyes wide as he took in the scene. Mallory strode in beside him, carrying her backpack. "Why is Mom putting jewelry on her backside? And what is that thing on your face, Dakota?"

Mallory stared at her sister. "Yeah, it's weird. And a little scary."

Dakota rolled her eyes. "It's called a smile, dummy, and Mom is joining the modern fashion age. She's going to throw out all her dowdy skirts and dress like a pop star. Sure it's jeggings at first, but then it's all corsets and leather pants."

Marcus laughed. "The day I see Mom in leather pants, I'll leave Texas forever."

"If we're doing a makeover for Mom, I'm in." Mallory set her backpack down and joined Dakota. "I think she needs the full Gaga."

"I was thinking more Katy Perry, with blue hair and confetti coming out of her bra," Dakota chimed in.

It was so good to see her kids smiling and laughing and happy.

Marcus put an arm around her. "I caught up with Mallory as she was heading to the library. I thought maybe since we're all together we could plan to go to lunch in a bit. Maybe invite along Ian."

"And me." Dillon strode back out. "I do not skip meals. Makes me hangry. Arrests go up and then everyone's cranky."

"I'm in." Tate patted his midsection. "I skipped breakfast. What do you say we hit the Bluebonnet and make me look like a man of the people. Which I am. I actually don't get that phrase."

"I don't either," Dakota said with a shake of her head. "What are you supposed to be, a man of the goats or something? Not that I haven't met a few of those. Starting with…"

"Dakota," Joanne interrupted as quickly as she could. "This would be a good place to practice that humility we talked about."

"Fine." Dakota groaned. "I'll go and eat at the Bluebonnet. I'm used to mostly ordering food there and sending it back because I don't eat. I might actually try something this time. If I'm going to work at a store that sells plus-sized clothes along with real actual clothes, who cares what size I am?"

Yes, she would have to work with Dakota on the humility thing.

"Awesome." Mallory leaned against Joanne. "That's double fries for me. No matter what she says, she's not really eating carbs. Can I maybe invite Luis?"

Her family just kept growing. "Of course. I better call and make sure they're ready for a party of our size."

Her party. Her family.

She turned to go and call the cafe when the door opened again.

"Hello, Joanne."

She felt the blood drain from her face. Hector was here. He was standing right there in the doorway of her office.

She stared at him and knew nothing would be the same again.

* * * *

Marcus felt every muscle in his body go tight as he turned and faced the man he had nightmares about.

Hector Alvarez strode in like he owned the place, like he wasn't the very last person any of them wanted to see.

"Daddy!" Dakota squealed and jumped off the desk, rushing to greet their father with a massive hug.

Maybe not everyone was unhappy to see him, but the man turned Marcus's stomach.

He felt his fist clench at his sides.

"Don't," his mother whispered. "Please don't do anything."

"Give me one reason."

"Because Tate is here and my job is on the line," she whispered. "Because I don't know what Hector will do if you start a fight. Please, Marcus. Please let me handle this."

This was why he'd left. This utter feeling of helplessness. Even now that he was a grown man with the physical strength to match that bully who'd fathered him, his mother wouldn't allow it. He had to sit by and watch as his mother went through hell. He couldn't do it.

Mallory slipped behind him.

At least one of the Alvarez females had some sense.

"It's going to be okay, Mal." He wasn't about to let that bastard hurt his sister. And if Hector made any move on his mother, he wouldn't let her pleas hold him back either.

He was well aware that they weren't alone. The three staffers his mom had hired came in from the back room, obviously unaware of the tense situation going on because they were chatting and laughing.

The three women looked up and suddenly they were talking behind their hands.

His mother was right about one thing. Whatever happened next would be gossiped about for weeks.

"Hector, I'm surprised to see you." Dillon had his hands on his hips, his fingers close to the gun at his belt.

"I bet you are," his father practically snarled.

"I'm so happy to see you, Daddy." Dakota beamed up at her father.

"I'm happy to see you, too, princess. You look good." Hector turned slightly, sending his gaze Mallory's way. "So do you, Mallory. You don't have a hug for your father?"

Mallory stiffened and then stepped away. "I'm due at the library. I'll see you later, Mom."

She practically ran out of the building.

That was one woman he didn't have to worry about.

As Mallory rushed out, Ian strode in. His eyes found Marcus, concern plain there. "Marcus, I found out…never mind. I take it this is your father."

"Yes, I am Marcus's father." Hector stared at Ian in a way that made Marcus think he was going to get violent at any moment. "This is my family. Who the hell are you?"

Ian bristled, stepping close to Marcus. "I'm the man who gave your son shelter when he ran away from home. Now I wonder why he would do that? Since his mother is such a nice lady, I have to think it wasn't her."

Tate was all smiles as he stepped in. "Now, this probably isn't the place for a family reunion. Hector, nice to see you. Welcome to my campaign office."

Hector reached out and shook the man's hand. "I heard you were running for mayor. I was surprised to hear my wife was your secretary."

Tate frowned. "She's not my secretary. She's running my campaign."

Hector laughed, a full-throated sound with just a hint of evil. "You have to be kidding me."

"She's running the campaign and she's doing an excellent job," Dillon said. The sheriff seemed to have grown an inch since Hector showed up. His tone had an arctic chill to it.

"I'm sure she is," Hector replied, "But I'm a little surprised she's not at home watching after her family. We have two girls who still need her and a son who's lost his way."

Oh, he could show Hector which way he'd found. "I think everything's been fine. You're the one who left without a word. Not that it hasn't been a pleasure…"

His mother held out a hand, reminding him they weren't alone. "I think we should probably put off lunch. Hector and I need to speak privately."

Hector winked the sheriff's way. "We definitely need to speak privately. It's been a long time since I saw my wife…privately. I need a little time with her."

"Sheriff, I would like to thank you for helping with moving the furniture around." His mother's voice had gone low, losing the new confidence and replaced with the soft tone he recognized from his childhood. She would use that tone of voice even while his vicious father beat the shit out of her. "But I need to handle some family business right now."

"Joanne," Dillon began.

"That's Mrs. Alvarez to you," Hector shot back. "Or have we lost all politeness in this town?"

"Of course not." Tate put a hand on the sheriff's shoulder. "Let's go get some lunch and leave the Alvarez clan to themselves. They need some time alone. Hector's been gone for a while. I'm sure he wants some family time."

Hector held his hand out to Joanne. "Damn straight I do. Joanne, your husband's been gone. Don't you think you should properly greet me?"

He watched his mother blanch, her body turning in on itself. Her shoulders hunched and she seemed to shrink before his eyes. But she didn't hesitate. She took Hector's hand and allowed him to drag her close. She tilted her head up and let him slam his mouth down on hers in a nasty version of a hello kiss.

Dillon cursed and slammed out of the building.

Marcus wasn't sure what was happening but the world started to take a red tone to it.

"Don't." Ian put a hand on his arm. "We've got eyes on us. Let your mother lead."

That was the trouble. His mother never led when it

came to his father. She simply allowed herself to be his punching bag. He wasn't sure he could watch that again and do nothing. He could feel the bile rising. His father was back and was useless again because no one would let him do what needed to be done—put that bastard in the ground where he belonged.

Hector came up for air and Marcus didn't miss the way his mother tried to move away from him. Hector caught her hand, holding it tight. "I think you'll understand why my wife needs the afternoon off, Tate. We need to…reconnect."

Tate averted his eyes. "Of course. Joanne, are you all right?"

She nodded. A smile that nowhere reached her eyes fluttered across her face. "Of course."

"She's just overwhelmed." Hector hauled her close. "Like I said, we've been separated for a while."

"He's been away." Dakota stepped in, putting a hand on Hector's shoulder. "But he's back now and everything is back to the way it should be."

His sister looked at their father like he was a conquering hero and not the abusive bastard he was, but then Hector had been careful around Dakota. Dakota was his favorite. She had never felt the hard edge of his hand.

I'll teach you how to be a man, boy. Even if it kills you. No son of mine is going to be a wussy.

"Thank you for the afternoon off," his mother was saying. She looked at Tate but her eyes seemed vacant. "I'll contact you later and let you know what's happening."

Tate stared for a moment but seemed to come to a decision. "You do that, Joanne. Call me if you need me. Hector, welcome home. I hope you know what an amazing woman you have there."

"I intend to let her know just what I think of her," Hector said, his lips turned up in a cruel approximation of a smile. "It's been a long time since I let my wife know that."

He was going to kill Hector. He was going to walk over and start in with his fists and he wouldn't let up until his father could no longer walk the earth.

Ian moved in front of him, placing his body between Marcus and Hector's. His voice was just a whisper but Marcus couldn't help but hear. "Stand down, son. You can't do a thing here but embarrass your mother more than she has been. I've been where you are and I understand. Go and cool off and then we'll talk."

One more person telling him what he couldn't do.

His mother was standing with that bastard like he had the right to claim her. Who the hell was he to argue?

"I've got things to do." All his plans, everything he'd worked for seemed like it had been a fool's errand. Why the hell had he left Montana at all?

His mother didn't even look at him.

Marcus walked out the door. It had all been for nothing and he'd been a fool to think things could ever change. Not here in Storm.

Chapter Four

Mallory forced herself to walk. She wanted to run. As fast and as far as she could. She wanted to run and never come back.

He was home. Her father was home.

She couldn't breathe. What was she going to do? Over the months he'd been gone she'd gotten used to a home where she felt safe, where she didn't have to hide or cover her ears, where she was able to be herself and it was okay.

Mallory looked to one side. Cuppa Joe's was to her left and she saw a couple of women staring at her. They shook their heads and the sympathy in their eyes made her want to throw up.

She marched on. Everyone knew and no one did a thing about it. That was the cruelest part of all. The people in the town would shake their heads but no one was going to save her mother.

"Hey," a familiar voice shouted.

Mallory turned and finally breathed a sigh of relief. Luis. He stood on the sidewalk looking like strength and comfort and safety all wrapped up in one beautiful boy. She couldn't help it. She knew she should get herself under control, but she ran to him.

Though his eyes showed confusion, he opened his arms, then wrapped them around her.

"What's going on?" He hugged her tight. "Mallory, what happened?"

She held on tight, not caring who was watching them. "My father…"

Luis gasped. "Oh, no. Did they find him? Is he gone?"

"Worse."

He sighed. "Then he's back. I'm so sorry. Is your mom all right?"

She sniffled and forced herself to pull away. She wasn't going to lose it right here in the middle of the town square. She looked up to see Marylee Rush staring at her, shaking her head like she was doing something wrong. Mallory ignored her. Marylee Rush thought everyone was trash. "My mom just accepted him. She didn't fight him or anything. I don't understand. I don't get it. Why won't she fight?"

Luis smoothed back her hair. "I don't know, but I'm sure it has something to do with you. I think your mother believes if she takes what your father has to give that he won't hurt you."

She shook her head. "I don't want him back in my life."

"I know." Luis looked to his left and his body stiffened.

She followed the line of his sight and her stomach turned once again. Her mother was walking out with her dad. He had a hand on her arm, practically dragging her behind him. Her mother just let herself get hauled along. At one point she stumbled and hit the ground. She could see the way her father forced her back up, the scowl on his face.

"Such a shame. That should not be displayed to the public. Family matters should be kept private." Marylee shook her head and that was when Mallory realized Brittany was with her grandmother.

"Hey, Mallory." The beautiful blonde stepped up, sympathy in her eyes. "Are you okay?"

She might never be okay again, but Mallory was well aware that she had eyes on her and Brittany was so important to her brother. She sucked it up and smiled. "I'm fine. My father is back. I think he and my mom have some things to talk about. That's all. You know how it is when a family member comes back after a long time."

She hoped Brittany didn't notice the fact that she was shaking. Shaking. She couldn't stop it.

Suddenly there was a warm, strong hand in hers. Luis was there, squeezing her fingers and making her realize she wasn't alone. He was here with her.

She took a deep breath and vowed to get through the next few moments.

"No, she doesn't because Brittany's family doesn't up and leave her for months at a time and then make a big scene when they come home," Marylee huffed.

"Grams, please." Brittany's cheeks went red.

Her father was dragging her mom to his car. Dakota was with them, shaking her head at their mom.

She'd been doing so well. The last few weeks Dakota had seemed almost human. Now she was sneering at their mom and beaming at their father and Marcus was nowhere to be seen.

Life was reverting to form, going back to what it had been when the last few months had almost been like paradise. She knew that was stupid. So much bad stuff had happened. She'd lost Lacey. Luis's sister, Ginny, had been caught in a scandal and yet Mallory had felt so free.

She wanted to talk to Lacey. There had been a time when nothing seemed real until she'd shared it with her best friend.

Luis's hand squeezed hers. Maybe she had a new best

friend.

"Well, I'm just saying that whole family has problems." Marylee wasn't backing down. "Would you look at that?"

Mallory watched in horror as Marcus emerged. Ian was by his side. They seemed to be talking for a moment and then Marcus saw their mother trip and fall to the ground. Their father seemed to say something to her. Mallory could guess.

You're so clumsy, Joanne. You're pathetic.

Marcus charged in, going for their father. Mallory heard Brittany gasp. Her brother looked like an angry bull ready to kill anyone in his path.

Marylee stepped in front of her granddaughter as though Marcus was coming after her.

Ian got between Marcus and his dad.

Luis tugged on her hand. "We need to go. Brittany, it was nice to see you."

She noted he pointedly didn't say the same to Brittany's grandmother, and Luis was always polite.

He was trying to save her. She let him lead her away, drawing her back toward Cuppa Joe's.

She followed him. The last thing she was going to do was go home.

* * * *

Brittany watched in horror as Hector Alvarez pulled his wife toward his car. He wasn't even pretending to help her. He simply dragged her along. Ian stopped Marcus from following, putting a hand on his chest. She could hear Joanne Alvarez telling Marcus that everything was fine.

Brittany started toward them, determined to stop what was happening before her eyes.

Her grandmother put a hand on her arm. "What are you doing?"

Mallory had just walked away, Luis's hand in hers. It had been obvious Marcus's little sister was emotionally distraught and there was no doubt about the cause. It looked like Hector Alvarez was back and he was making himself known.

She needed to go and be with Marcus. Maybe she would calm him down or maybe she would help him beat the crap out of his father.

"Well, that was inevitable." Her father, Senator Sebastian Rush, joined them. He'd been parking the car and Brit was happy he'd missed talking to Mallory and Luis. It would have only made Mallory feel worse. "What a nasty scene. How many people do you think saw it?"

Her grandmother shook her head, keeping a hand on Brittany. "At least ten people, but you know they're all on their phones right now so everyone will know about it soon."

"Grams, let me go. I need to talk to Marcus." Brittany felt sick as she watched Joanne climb into the back seat of Hector's car while Dakota claimed the front. She had a grin on her face like the cat who'd gotten all the cream.

Her father stepped up. "Absolutely not. You're not getting involved in that mess, and now I have to talk to Tate because it happened right in front of his campaign office."

Marcus stood and watched the car with his mother driving away. The look on his face nearly broke her heart.

Marylee turned to her. "I know how you feel about that boy, but I need you to think about your family right now." She looked around as though trying to see if anyone was watching them. She seemed satisfied that all eyes were on Marcus because she spoke again. "Your father barely won reelection. I know you're angry with him but his job is important to this family. Think about your mother."

"It wasn't barely," her father complained. "It was two whole points. That's fairly respectable, but yes, you should think of your mother, Brittany."

She thought about her mother all the time. She couldn't understand why her mother hadn't walked out. It was something she and Marcus had in common. They didn't understand their parents' marriages. But they both loved their moms very much.

"It looks like the boy has some support," her father said. "If you walk up to him right now our name is going to get embedded into that story and we've already had enough gossip around this family to last forever."

She stared at her father, the hypocrite. All that gossip had been about him and his bad behavior. "Are you serious?"

He shrugged. "Just because it was about me doesn't make it any less true. I know you're still angry with me, Brittany, but you don't want to hurt your mother and brother. Jeffry can't handle more of this. He's been bullied about his family. Let's not bring the sins of the Alvarez family into his life."

She wasn't sure her brother had been directly bullied, but she knew he'd felt the heat of having everyone in town speculating about their family and making judgments. It had been a terrible time and this had the potential to start all the talk up again. They would ask what Hector would do to her father now that he was back in town. If she was seen with Marcus right now, it really would drag her family into it.

"Come along," her grandmother said. "We should skip lunch and head home. This is all anyone will talk about and I don't want to have anything to do with it."

"And you shouldn't have anything to do with that boy," her father said. "Not while he's living under Hector Alvarez's roof. That man is dangerous and everyone knows it."

"Then why don't people help Joanne?"

Her father's shoulders moved in an elegant shrug. "It

isn't our business. If the woman wanted help, she would ask for it. I'm sure the sheriff would be more than happy to deal with the problem for her."

Marylee shook her head. "Yes, that's obvious. Another scandal waiting to explode. That family is full of them. At least we only have to deal with your father. The rest of our family is solid. Every single Alvarez seems to have trouble. And that one inherited his father's temper."

She was looking at Marcus, who had his fists clenched at his sides as he talked to Ian Briggs. He stood right outside Tate Johnson's campaign office, still glued to the spot where he'd watched his mother hauled away by his father while everyone who happened to be on the square stared at them.

Hector had been the reason Marcus left for Montana the first time. Would he leave again? Would she even get a good-bye? She couldn't stand the thought of not having that man in her life. No matter what her family said.

"Have you thought about the fact that he could hurt you?" Her grandmother's lips were a flat line, her eyes full of deep concern.

"Marcus would never hurt me." She knew it in her soul. She stared across the square, across the distance that separated them, and wanted so badly to run to him.

"I'm sure that's what Joanne said before she married Hector," her father shot back, his distaste evident. His loafers tapped against the concrete sidewalk, a sure sign he was getting impatient. "I'm sure she didn't see that side of him until after he had a ring on her finger. But the truth is already known about that one. He's violent and he has the record to prove it."

All those arrests. He'd explained them. She believed him. Marcus would never hurt her. Never.

Had Joanne thought that, too, once? Had she gone into her marriage with the conviction that her husband loved her, would treat her like a princess? She was sure Joanne had never dreamed of a day when he would humiliate her in front of the entire town.

Marcus turned and his eyes flared, catching hers. Longing. She could see it in his eyes. He started toward her and then stopped as her father stepped in front of her. His face fell, but he stood watching her as though offering her a choice.

To go to him. To comfort him.

"It's time to go." Marylee turned on her heels.

"You two head home," her father announced. "I've got one last bit of business to take care of."

He was likely going to talk to Tate, to further make Joanne's life miserable.

Brittany turned away. She had to think of her family. Though it made her ache inside, she would have to talk to Marcus later.

She got into the car feeling lower than ever.

Chapter Five

Ginny hurried along the street. She'd seen what had happened with Marcus and the way he'd stared after Brittany. Ginny's heart ached for her friend, but she couldn't stand the thought of the senator seeing her and sneering at her. Or worse.

She walked down the side street toward her sister's car with the cake in hand. Marisol was busy and Ginny didn't have the heart to tell her sister that Luis was seeing Mallory on the sly. Especially not when she knew what Mallory must be going through. Mallory needed Luis and she wasn't about to put up one more barrier for them.

She knew what it felt like to need a hand in hers. Sometimes she woke up in the middle of the night and she could swear she could still feel Logan's fingers squeezing her own, giving her strength. She could see him smiling down at her and telling her that they were going to be a family soon.

And then she woke up and he had nothing but anger for her.

She was glad Marisol parked on a side street. Back in the square there would still be people watching, milling around, and gossiping like the Alvarez family woes were nothing more than a show put on for their entertainment.

It made her angry.

She took a deep breath. She needed to stay calm. For her baby.

"Do you need help with that, Ginny?"

She froze because she knew that voice. It haunted her dreams, too, though the ones he occupied were more like nightmares.

She gently placed the cake on the floorboard in the back seat of the car where it couldn't get ruined and turned to the senator. She wanted to open the driver's door, get in, and drive away, but she hadn't been fast enough.

How had she ever thought this man handsome? He turned her stomach now. Senator Sebastian Rush stood there in his expensive suit, his hair styled and tie perfectly tied. He was a Barbie doll of a man. Nothing like Logan. "I think you should get back to your family, Senator."

He put a hand on the car, leaning in. "My family is exactly why I thought we should talk."

She was stuck unless she wanted to walk away from the car. "I have work to do."

"So do I, no thanks to you," he said with a frown.

"I'm not the one who stood in front of the whole town and aired all our dirty laundry." She was guilty of many things, but that wasn't one of them.

"It doesn't matter. You're the one who got pregnant." He looked down at her belly.

She put a hand over it, as though she could protect her baby from him. "I didn't do it alone."

"No, but you certainly could have taken care of it alone."

She shivered at the thought of what he would have

wanted her to do. If things had happened differently, would she have gone to him? Asked him for advice? Or would she have simply gone to Jacob and told him she was pregnant? Probably the latter since she hadn't developed a backbone then. She was trying to have one now. "I am alone and I will take care of my baby alone."

The senator sneered, but finally stepped back. "If only we still had that choice."

"What do you mean?"

"I mean every day that goes by, your belly gets bigger and I get more questioning looks."

"Ignore them. I do."

"I was barely reelected and it was only because the competition didn't have enough time to truly find a worthy candidate. I've got this term to figure out how to mitigate the damage you caused."

"I caused?"

"You're the one who decided it was a good idea to have that child."

"What exactly was I supposed to do?" She shook her head. "I know what you wished I'd done. I'm sure it's how you would have handled it, but this is my life and my baby. You don't have to have anything to do with us. I prefer it that way."

"And when the child is told who its father is? How will you handle that, Ginny? Do you think the town gossips will keep their mouths closed? Do you think they'll all keep silent because that's what's best for your baby? You're naïve. As soon as it's old enough to understand, there'll be whispers about it. Some child will overhear and tell it what his momma said and then the child will want to know why I'm not around. Even before the baby is old enough, the town will want to know why I ignore a child who is obviously mine."

"Maybe the baby won't look like you. Maybe my child

will look like Jacob." She knew the words were stubborn, knew there was very little chance, but she still prayed for this baby in her belly to be Jacob's, to be a Salt. Not that she would love her baby less, but because she could tell her baby that he or she had been conceived in kindness and caring.

She no longer fooled herself that she'd been in love with Jacob. Now that she'd been close to Logan, she knew what real love was, but what she'd felt for Jacob had been pure in its way.

She felt nothing but contempt for the man in front of her.

He looked around as though assuring himself that no one was coming. "I would dearly love to believe that, but we both know it's futile. That boy couldn't sire children and I'm perfectly capable. When that child is toddling around this town looking like a clone of me, how am I going to handle that?"

"I really don't care. It's none of my business how you handle anything at all."

His eyes narrowed, gaze sharpening on her. "So you're not intending to come after me for child support, then?"

She shook her head. "Not at all. I want nothing from you except to be left alone."

"It won't solve the problem. Neither will paying you child support. This is a small town. I'll always be looked on as the man who got a girl pregnant and walked away from his responsibilities. I survived this, but next time they'll see an actual child and they'll question my morality."

Ginny didn't question his morality at all. She was certain he had no morals. "That's your problem, Senator. Now if you don't mind, I have to get back to work. I have a cake to deliver."

And a baby to support.

She was pleased at how well she'd handled herself. She

hadn't dissolved into tears. She'd faced him and told him what she thought. Maybe she was growing up after all.

"Of course, most people will forgive a man if he turns his life around." The senator wasn't looking directly at her. His eyes were on the distance, as though his brain was working on the problem and he wasn't actually seeing what was in front of him.

"I hope that you do." For Brittany and Jeffry's sake.

His gaze came back to her. "Sometimes a man has to change the optics of the situation. Do you understand what I mean when I talk about optics?"

"It's the way people see a topic." She wasn't sure where he was going with this, but she didn't need him to define political terms.

"It's the way the media specifically covers a topic. Right now I'm the villain. I'm the one who used a young girl and tossed her aside. Just because I have nothing further to do with you doesn't mean I shouldn't still care for my child, for the little baby that has my blood. If I gave that child my name and my protection, that changes the optics. Suddenly I'm merely a father trying to do right by his child."

Ginny couldn't breathe. He couldn't mean what he was saying. "You wouldn't."

He couldn't come after her baby. This was her child. She wasn't going to allow Sebastian Rush to come in and take her baby so he would look good in the press. He couldn't possibly think of using her child as a political pawn.

But then wasn't that what he'd tried to do with Logan?

If he came after her in a custody fight, how would she handle it? She didn't have any money.

He stepped back. "I don't know. I'm certainly not saying I would, but I like to keep my options open. It's something I have to think about, but you don't have all the cards in this game, Ginny Moreno, so don't think you've won a damn thing yet."

He turned and strode down the street. Ginny watched him, her heart beating against her chest.

Had she thought she only felt contempt for the man? Now her overwhelming emotion about him was fear.

* * * *

Marcus watched as Brittany walked away, her grandmother at her side. The senator took a different path, but Marcus was sure he was wholeheartedly behind Brittany's choice to leave without speaking to him.

"Are you all right?" Ian asked. "I'm sorry, that was a stupid question. Of course you're not all right."

"No, but I'm not going to jail for murder, thanks to you. I wish I'd known Brittany was watching me."

"What?" Ian peered down the road where Marylee was hustling Brittany into their car. "Damn. That's not good. I guess the whole town saw that scene."

"No way they missed it." And from the horror on Tate Johnson's face, Marcus had to wonder if his mother wasn't about to lose her job.

Not that Hector the Horrible would let her keep it.

Why had he come back? Why hadn't Marcus's prayers been answered and he was buried in a shallow grave somewhere?

Had Brittany seen him almost lose control? That was wrong. He had lost control. Ian had been the only reason he hadn't attacked his father.

"Are they gone? Did he take Joanne with him?" The sheriff strode up, his face an angry red. It looked like Tate had only been able to keep him away for so long. His boots thudded against the concrete, a frustrated sound.

"I need you to stay calm, son. I know you're angry, but you need to talk to your mother and figure out how she wants this handled." Ian seemed intent on being the voice of reason.

"You saw how she handled it." Like she always did.

"She went with him?" Dillon's eyes closed as if a pain had suddenly come over his body. "She left with him?"

"Of course she did." It was what his mother did. She placated the beast.

"That's not what I saw," Ian insisted. "I saw a woman who didn't want her family argument to be talked about for the next ten years. She wasn't happy to see him. She was just trying to make the best of a bad situation. She'll talk to him when they've got some privacy."

"You don't know my mother." His heart ached. Not only had his mother reverted to form, but Brittany had turned away from him.

Maybe she was right to do it. Hector was back in town. He poisoned everything he touched, and that included Marcus. It wouldn't matter that he would have nothing to do with the man. Hector would find a way to ruin everything Marcus wanted and loved. He would find a way to twist it so it turned on Marcus. Even Brittany.

Dillon turned to him. "No, Ian's right. Your mother was trying to avoid a scene."

"Well, she failed. She tripped and dear old dad just railed at her and forced her up. It was horrible and everyone saw it. He was pulling her along. It had nothing to do with clumsiness."

"I know that and so does most of this town," Dillon insisted. "Look, your mother has changed over the last few months. She's grown and she's so much stronger than she was. She's been happy. I don't think she's going to throw that away now."

"The minute he walked in, she gave up." He knew his mother.

"No, she tried to keep the peace." Ian put a hand on his shoulder. "She was in the middle of her office. She couldn't have it out with him. You need to have some faith in her."

Was Ian right? His mother had changed in the last few months. She'd blossomed and his world had been better for it. She'd taken charge of her life when there was no longer a husband around to ruin it for her. She'd smiled more and laughed more in the past couple of months than in all the years of his childhood.

Surely she wouldn't throw that away.

His cell phone buzzed in his pocket. "I hope so. I should probably get home."

He pulled it out of his jeans.

"I'll go with you. I don't like the thought of him being alone with her." Dillon took a deep breath. "I definitely think we should head over to the house."

It was a text from Brittany. He swiped his finger across the screen to read it.

I'm so sorry. I didn't want to cause a scene with my grandmother. Let's try to meet up later. In private.

In private. In secret. So her parents didn't know. It made his gut ache, but he understood.

His father was a monster. Who wanted to have that stain on them? He certainly didn't want it on his Brittany. She was too sweet to ever expose her to his father.

How had things seemed to be coming together this morning? How had he woken up and smiled and known that his world was going the right way for once? He'd had the ranch and his girl. He'd made plans to build a house he might one day share with her.

In an instant it had all changed and now he stared down at his phone.

"Are you going to call her?" Ian asked. "Because I do think we should get over to your house as soon as we can."

"We need to support your mom," Dillon said, conviction in his voice.

He turned the phone off. He wasn't going to call her. Not today. "Let's go."

He started toward his car, ready to face the monster from his childhood.

Chapter Six

"I'm so happy to have you back, Daddy." Dakota practically bounced in her seat.

At least one person in the world was happy to have him back. Hector made the turn that would take them home. Just a few moments more and he might be able to get his wife alone. He had a lot to say to her. "I'm very happy to see you, too, baby girl. I've missed you."

He looked in the rearview mirror and caught sight of his wife. He'd stared at her through the glass door of Tate Johnson's campaign office for a few moments before he'd gone in, and just briefly, she'd looked as pretty as she had on the day they married. She'd been smiling and laughing and he'd remembered why he'd asked her to be his wife.

Then he realized she'd been smiling for that bastard Dillon Murphy and his gut had clenched. Murphy had stood in there with Hector's children all around him and acted like he belonged there.

"Are you going to tell us why you left?" Dakota asked, her voice small.

His girl. She was Daddy's little girl. The only one of his kids Joanne hadn't managed to turn away from him. She'd been up to her old tricks the minute they'd left the building. He'd tried to take her hand and the clumsy bitch had fallen. He'd started to think she did it on purpose. She'd managed it just as Marcus had come out, and naturally his son thought the worst of him.

That's what his mother had taught him to think.

It was time to take control of his family again.

"I'll talk about it when the time is right, but for now I want to enjoy being back together with my favorite girl." He looked back at Joanne. It was good for her to know that she wasn't his favorite. She needed to know her place, and it looked like he would have to teach her all over again. "The first thing I need to do is try to get my job back. I have a family to take care of. I'm sure we're behind on bills."

"No, we're not. I've taken care of most of it and Marcus helped with the rest," Joanne said quietly.

"And just what have you been doing that you managed that?"

Dakota piped up. "She got a job. It's kind of weird and I don't get why she's the one to do it, but they paid her better than the flower shop. She worked for Marylee Rush before that whole family lost its mind and then Tate hired her."

Had Tate Johnson been fucking around with his wife? He couldn't imagine anything she was actually good at, but she was passably pretty and some men would pay for it. "What exactly did you do for Tate?"

"Silly stuff, from what I can tell. She folds a lot of pamphlets with his face on them," Dakota said as he turned into their driveway.

"I'm his campaign manager." Joanne didn't move as he put the car in park.

It was completely ridiculous. His wife couldn't manage

the house much less some politician's campaign. "I just bet you are. You should understand we're going to have a discussion about that. I don't like you working for some other man."

"I had to have a job. I had to make more money. You didn't leave us with any."

"Well, you pushed him out," Dakota said. "What did you expect him to do? Should he keep on sending you all his money even after you were awful to him?"

"Could we please have this argument inside?" Joanne asked. "People are watching."

He looked around and she was right. There were a couple of their neighbors out in the yard, staring at the car. Likely they'd been notified by their friends, who'd seen them in the town square.

Dakota opened her door. "Old biddies. They need to get a life."

Hector got out. There was a time and place for everything and his wife had been making a spectacle of herself far too often it seemed to him. It was time she understood that he was back and he was in charge.

She'd let Dakota run wild while he was gone. He blamed her for Dakota getting involved in that mess. If she hadn't been out playing around at her so called job, maybe she would have noticed that Dakota was being taken advantage of. He got out and grabbed his bag, all the while feeling eyes on him.

Joanne had done this. She'd brought the gossips down on their head with her whining and her uselessness, and maybe she'd done it with her faithlessness.

If he found out she'd been sleeping around, he might strangle her himself. What the hell good was a faithless woman?

Joanne emerged from the back seat. She wouldn't look him in the eye. "Why don't we go inside?"

"Why don't you tell me why you were with Dillon Murphy?"

Her cheeks flushed. "I wasn't with him. He gave me a ride into town and then he helped me move some furniture that was too heavy for me to move."

A ride into town? "Since when is the town's law enforcement a taxi service? Did you call him?"

"Please, can we go inside?"

He growled his frustration. She always had to have things her way. He strode up and Dakota was unlocking the door. He followed her inside.

His house. The one he'd purchased. It was good to be home. He'd spent months and month in hellholes and all because that bastard Dillon Murphy had run him out of town.

Did Joanne know what her friend had done? Were they still only friends or had Murphy managed to convince her to be something more. Joanne was weak. She could be led. Most women could, as evidenced by his own sweet daughter's troubles.

"Now we're inside. Do you want to explain what you were doing with the sheriff?"

Joanne closed the door behind her. "I told you. He was only helping me with moving the furniture."

"He comes by all the time, Daddy," Dakota said. "It's annoying. He was here this morning for breakfast."

He felt his rage rise.

"He was just passing by. He's checked in on me since you left." Joanne's voice pleaded with him. "It's nothing."

He couldn't hit her in front of Dakota, but he could feel his fist clenching. It had been too long since she'd felt his power. Dakota wasn't the only one who was running wild. He was going to change that. "It doesn't sound like nothing. It sounds like you've been having a very good time in my absence."

She looked up at him. "Of course not. It's been hard and you didn't bother to tell me you were leaving."

"I don't owe you any explanations." Had she really wondered? She wasn't a good liar. He could always see straight through her, which made him pause now. "In fact, I'm pretty sure you know exactly why I left."

She shook her head. "I have no idea. Why would I know that?"

"It was probably because you're so clumsy." Dakota sat down on the sofa. "It's annoying. I know I've often thought I need a vacation from how annoying Mom can be."

"Why don't you grab a beer for me, sweetheart?" If he could get Joanne alone for a few moments, he would show her how he felt.

Dakota rolled her eyes. "Mom doesn't let Marcus have any beer. No one gets to have fun when she's in charge."

Marcus allowed her to tell him what he could and couldn't do? His boy was a pansy ass and he wanted to know who the man was who'd pretended to be his father. He'd gotten in between him and Marcus when his boy had finally shown some proof he might be a man.

"Hector, I have no idea why you left. You didn't tell me," Joanne argued. She managed to keep her tone quiet, but he knew stubbornness when he heard it. "You just walked out. I had to get a job. I had to try to keep our house. Why would you think I knew why you left?"

He stared at her for a moment, assessing her. She didn't know what Murphy had done? It seemed that was the truth. Murphy had left her out.

Perhaps his fist wasn't his only weapon.

"Ugh," Dakota said. "Here he comes again. I told you he's here all the time. I think he's friends with Marcus or something. I just don't know why anyone would want to be friends with a sheriff."

Sure enough he looked out the front window and

Dillon Murphy was walking up to his porch. He was followed by Marcus and that other ass.

The gang was all here. Maybe it was time to let Joanne know what had really been going on.

* * * *

Ginny knocked on Francine Hoffman's door and prayed the nurse was home. What kind of hours did she work? She might be at the hospital at this time of day.

She couldn't risk going to the hospital. Someone might see her and then the talk would start up. They would wonder if something was wrong with the baby.

The Rushes would use anything they could against her. Her hands were shaking as she went to knock again.

Before she could manage it, the door opened and Francine was there, looking crisp and clean in her scrubs, her hair back as though she was getting ready for work. Her brown eyes sparkled as she smiled. "Well, hello, Ginny. I wasn't expecting you."

Ginny nodded. "I'm so sorry. I should have called, but I had to talk to you."

Francine sobered, seeming to sense that something was wrong. She opened the door, allowing Ginny to enter. "Of course. Is there something wrong with the baby? Do we need to get you to the hospital?"

Ginny walked into Francine's house. It was tidy, but lived in. The whole place had warmth to it. "I'm fine. Little Bit's fine, too. For now. I have to ask you if you've gotten the tests back yet."

She wasn't giving up hope. Not until she had it completely confirmed. A few weeks back she'd asked Francine to run a paternity test on Little Bit. It hadn't been easy, but they'd done it, and they'd managed to keep it quiet.

She had to know if Jacob was the father. If the test

came back negative, well, then she would know who her baby's dad was and she might have a fight on her hands.

Francine offered her a seat. "I told you it's going to take some time to get the results back. I had to send it out of state for testing and I had to pull some strings even then. We don't want it leaked to the press that you're getting a paternity test done."

That was the last thing she wanted. If she never had press attention again for the rest of her life, it would be far too soon. "I'm sorry. I'm just very eager to see the results."

Francine studied her for a moment. "Honey, what's going on? It's easy to see you're upset."

She was beyond upset. She was barely keeping it together, but she had to because there was no way she was causing more gossip. "I'm fine, just anxious about the results."

Francine leaned forward, putting a hand on her arm. "Did something happen?"

She hated the way the world went blurry. She needed to be strong.

"Come on, Ginny," Francine cajoled. "If something's happened, you need to talk about it."

"It's about the senator. I don't want to put you in any more of a bad position than I already have."

She shook her head. "I might be friends with Payton, but I'm friends with you, too. What we discuss won't leave here. I certainly haven't told her anything about the tests we've run. Those are for you and the results are strictly for you. You can choose or not choose to share them with whoever you like. This is your body and your baby, Ginny. And that means you have to take care of yourself right now. Stress is bad for your system. You need to talk about it. If not with me, then someone else."

She didn't have anyone else. She couldn't burden her sister any more than she already had and her best friend no longer spoke to her. She missed Brittany so much, but it was another relationship she'd screwed up. "I think the senator might come after my baby."

Francine sighed and sat back. "Is that all? Sweetheart, there's not a man alive who is less paternal than Sebastian Rush. Don't get me wrong. He's not terrible to the children he has, but he also didn't exactly raise them. That was left to Payton. He's certainly not going to sue you for custody of another child. Believe me. Brittany and Jeffry have only ever been stage pieces for that man. He brings them out when the occasion calls for him to look like a family man."

"I know that." She'd heard it from Brittany many times. Her father only really saw her and Jeffry as a way to show the world he was a good family man.

"Then relax because you should know he's not going to run around parading his love child in front of the press." She sent a sympathetic look Ginny's way.

There had been no love between the two of them, just a young girl seeking affection and wanting to feel like a woman for once. "He thinks if he takes care of his bastard child, maybe the voters will forgive him."

Francine paled. "No. He wouldn't. Marylee wouldn't allow it. I know Payton would never take that child from you."

"They might not have a choice in the matter, and I think Marylee might if she thought it would rehab her son's image."

"I don't see how it could do that. I should think he would want to hide it, keep quiet so people would stop talking about it."

"Will they? Will they ever stop talking about it?" Ginny felt so tired. "Or will the gossips keep finding reasons to bring it up? They'll talk about it again when my baby is born. It'll come up with every man I ever date. When the senator runs for reelection, the story will make the rounds again. I don't think it will ever really go away."

"I know it seems like it won't. But people really do forget. In a few months, the senator will go back to Austin and he'll get back to work. You'll settle down and raise your baby and life will go on."

"Until the next election cycle. I'll always be brought up when he's running for office. He's an ambitious man. I don't think he'll be happy in his current position forever. He's going to want more." She'd been savaged by the local and state press. What would she do on a national stage? How would she ever be able to survive it?

What if he decided to run for president?

Francine shook her head. "I guess I hadn't thought about it that way. I think you're going to have to keep your head down and hope for the best. You have to worry about your baby now. Everything else is a bridge you'll cross when you come to it."

A bridge that could fall out from under her and send her into the canyon below. "Everything would change if the test proved Jacob is my baby's father."

"You know the likelihood of that is very slim. Jacob's injuries left him with little to no chance of ever fathering a child. I could go into all the medical reasons for it but that's the truth."

She hung on to the only words that mattered. "But what if it's more of the little chance portion of that diagnosis and not the no chance?"

"The percentage chance is very low, Ginny."

"But it's not zero." She needed a miracle now more than ever.

"No, it's not zero," Francine conceded. "That's the only reason I let you talk me into this test. You're never going to be satisfied until you know. I understand that. But it's still going to be a few weeks. So you need to rest and put this out of your mind."

"I don't see how, but I'll try." She stood up. It was time to put on a happy face and get back to Cuppa Joe's. It wouldn't do to let Marisol know how upset she was. There was nothing her sister could do but worry along with her. "Please let me know as soon as you hear anything."

"I promise I will." Francine hugged her. "The minute I get those tests back, I'll call you. It's going to be all right, Ginny."

Ginny wished she could believe her.

Chapter Seven

Joanne winced when the door opened and Marcus stepped inside. She'd hoped for more time before she had to deal with her son.

He'd been so angry. She'd seen it in Marcus's eyes. He'd been ready to hurt Hector right there in the middle of the town square and she'd known then and there that she would do anything to spare him the aftermath of such violence.

He'd already gotten in trouble for his temper. He'd been arrested and she couldn't stand the thought of Dillon having to arrest her baby boy and put him in jail. She wasn't going to let Hector win that way.

She put on her brightest smile because Marcus hadn't come alone. He'd brought Ian and Sheriff Murphy with him. Dillon. He looked so solid. She wanted to walk right up to him and wrap her arms around him. She wanted to go back to that moment when he'd kissed her and never leave it. Just let that one moment last forever.

How was she going to survive the next few hours? The next days? There would be no more Dillon Murphy to save her. Not after what she had to do. She gave them all a tremulous smile.

"Hi, guys. I'm so sorry about that stuff in the square. It all went a little crazy out there. You didn't understand, Marcus. I tripped. That had nothing to do with your father." Except he'd been pulling her so hard, she couldn't keep up. She'd tried because she'd known everyone was watching them, but she'd stumbled at the curb and he hadn't noticed for a second.

Her knee still ached, but she wasn't about to complain. Certainly not now that Marcus and Dillon were here. She wished Marcus hadn't brought Dillon and Ian along. She actually wished she could talk to Hector alone.

Except she was also afraid of being alone with him. She knew that look in his eyes. The minute he got her alone, he would take out his aggressions on her. He was a bomb waiting to go off, but if he did it in front of Marcus, that bomb would suddenly be nuclear.

She couldn't let her son go to jail. And she was too ashamed to let Dillon see how her husband really treated her.

"Sure, Mom," Marcus said, his eyes going straight to his father. "You tripped. I've never heard that one before."

"You always were such a clumsy idiot," Dakota said with a shake of her head. "It's embarrassing. I'm sure it was all anyone could talk about today. I've had to deal with it all my life. I've been bullied over how clumsy you are."

All that hard work right down the drain. It hadn't taken Dakota ten minutes to go right back to the brat she'd been before her father left. The minute her father had walked in the room, Dakota had forgotten everything she'd learned over the last several months. She was right back to the selfish, narcissistic child she'd always been.

"Joanne, did he hurt you?" Dillon asked, his eyes taking on that steely glare she always saw when he was doing his job.

Why couldn't anyone stay calm? She knew Dillon would make a big deal out of it. It was why she'd been so happy when he'd walked away. "I'm fine. There's nothing to worry about. Hector and I simply need to talk."

Alone. She had to be brave. She had to face her husband.

Oh, why had he come back? Why was he here? She wanted to wake up. She prayed this was all just a nightmare.

"Why don't we sit down and talk this out?" Ian asked reasonably.

He didn't understand that Hector wasn't reasonable.

"Why don't you get out of my house and mind your own business, asshole?" Hector shot back.

"Good one, Dad." Dakota never let up. She would stoke the flames until they became a massive wildfire.

Marcus frowned, his hands at his sides. "Don't talk to him that way. He's my boss."

"What does he have you doing? I thought you were working at the Johnson Ranch." Hector proved that even though he'd been gone he still knew what was happening.

Who had been filling him in? Had he been watching her all this time? She'd come to believe that she was safe, but had he been out there all along just waiting for the right moment to strike? She wouldn't put anything past him.

"I'm moving some of my business down here. Marcus is going to run the Texas ranch." Ian crossed his arms over his chest. "You should know that I watch out for my employees. I consider them family."

Joanne put herself between Hector and Ian because she knew exactly how he would respond. He didn't like anyone questioning him. Never. He definitely didn't like anyone coming between him and something he thought he owned. She understood that Ian thought he was being helpful, but she knew how to handle Hector. She was likely the only one who knew how to get out of this without someone going to jail. "Ian took Marcus in when he landed in Montana. He gave Marcus a job and took care of him when we couldn't."

"You mean when he ran away like a whining boy?" Hector asked.

Ian's chest swelled. "I think he was more like a scared boy. You should watch out because that boy's become a man."

Hector's eyes narrowed. "Has he now? Are you the one who turned my boy into a man? I'd like to know just how you did that. What exactly is your relationship with my son?"

"Stop it," Joanne said and then realized what she'd done. She averted her eyes out of habit. "I'm sorry. Could we please stop arguing? Ian is a good man. He took care of Marcus when we couldn't."

"Don't act like he gave a crap, Mom." Marcus was staring at his father like he was ready to continue what he'd started on the square.

She couldn't allow that to happen. Hector could kill Marcus and not think twice about it. Marcus wouldn't know when to stop, wouldn't know when things had gone too far and he had to give in. "You don't understand him. Marcus, when you're young you often don't see things as they truly are."

"Oh, he sees things quite clearly," Dillon said.

"Marcus has always been a troublemaker. He's always clashing with Daddy." Dakota watched the action with a smug smirk on her face. "And he ran away to get attention."

"I didn't want his attention, Dakota. I was sick of his attention. I left because this family is toxic. We were doing great, you know." Marcus took a step toward his father. "We were fine. Mom is better than ever and even Dakota was halfway tolerable. We don't need you here. Why don't you go back to wherever you came from?"

"Marcus," Joanne admonished.

"Are you seriously going to just let him walk right back in here like nothing happened?" Marcus asked, anguish in his tone. "Do you have any idea what he's been doing while he left you all alone with nothing? He took all the cash and you had to take care of us. What was he doing? How many women did you have on the side, Dad? Did you spend all the money on one of them? Did she finally get sick of you and throw you out? Is that why you slithered home? You thought Mom would take you back? Well, I'm here to tell you she doesn't need you anymore. So get out."

Oh, she understood what her son was trying to do and she loved him for it. Unfortunately, she also knew it wouldn't work. Maybe Dillon's presence right now would keep Hector at bay, but Dillon couldn't be around all the time. Hector would take out all his rage on Marcus when he least expected it. A vision of her son dead by his father's hand assaulted her.

She had to do what she'd always done. She had to calm the situation down and then allow Hector to vent that rage on her. Not her children. Never her children.

Then she would figure out what to do.

"Marcus, you don't speak for me."

Marcus turned startled eyes her way. "You can't mean to welcome him back."

"He's my husband." The words came easily, out of long practice. It was funny how simple it was to fall into old patterns. They'd been her refuge, her only way to get through the everyday horrors of her marriage. She told herself she loved him. She had to since she married him.

Or you made a mistake and it's time you forgave yourself.

She tried to close off that tiny voice inside her that had started speaking in the last few weeks. It was the voice that she'd suppressed ever since the first time Hector used his fist to shut her up.

The voice had started to whisper again. And then to

talk. And now it was shouting.

What are you doing? Fight back. You have something good going with Dillon. Who cares what everyone else will think? That's a man who takes you seriously. He believes in you. He wouldn't lie to you or manipulate you. Trust in him. Believe in yourself.

"You want to know why I left?" Hector looked to her, reaching out and taking her hand. "I left because the sheriff threatened to kill me."

She felt her jaw drop. "That's ridiculous."

Hector squeezed her hand just to the point of pain, but his expression was soft, almost apologetic. It was what he was good at—showing her his brute power while fooling the world around them. "No, it's not. He came to me the day of Jacob Salt's funeral and threatened to shoot me. How had you set that up, Sheriff? You'll have to remind me. That beating I took from you was pretty harsh. I think you were going to plant drugs on me, right? That was how you would justify killing me."

It was one of Hector's tricks. He was obviously trying to cover for exactly what Marcus had accused him of. She'd spent many a long night since Hector had abandoned them wondering what he was up to. She suspected he'd found another woman, a younger one. There had been nights she'd cursed that woman, though lately she'd started to pray for her.

She looked to Dillon, ready to send him an apologetic look.

He'd turned a deep red, his jaw tight. She knew that look. It was the look of a guilty man.

"Dillon?"

"Joanne, I was only looking out for you." His words were soft, pleading.

Joanne's world tilted and turned. Dillon was supposed to be the one who didn't lie to her. He was upstanding. He was the sheriff.

"How could you?" She couldn't look at him.

Hector brought her hand up to his chest, holding it close. "He beat me pretty badly, Joanne. I'm so sorry. I had to leave in order to protect you and our girls."

"How could you?" Dakota had to put her two cents in. "We're going to get a lawyer and sue you and your department. If you think you won't lose your job over this, you're crazy."

"I have to talk to you, Joanne," Dillon insisted.

"Did you or did you not threaten my husband?" Her heart was breaking. Please let him say it was all a mistake and Hector was lying. Maybe she could find the strength to deal with this if Hector was lying again.

Dillon was silent for a moment and then he nodded his head. "But I did it for you. Can't you see..."

She cut him off. "Get out of my house."

Marcus shook his head. "Mom, you have to listen to him. If he did it, it was for your own good."

She was so sick of hearing that. And if she let him stay, he would likely pick a fight with his father and she wasn't sure she could handle that tonight. "Marcus, I think you should take some time to cool off. When you can speak to your father in a respectful tone, you're welcome to come back."

It was the only way she knew to save him. Hector would never hurt Dakota and Mallory was too smart to put herself in a position where he would physically harm her. Marcus wasn't. He would fight and push and eventually Hector would explode.

As for Dillon, well, she didn't even want to think about him.

He'd lied to her. All the times she'd asked if he knew where Hector had gone, he'd looked her right in the eye and lied. How could she possibly trust him again?

"Joanne," Dillon began.

Marcus put a hand up. "Don't bother. This is what she does. She thinks I left the first time because I couldn't stand to be around my father and that's right mostly. What she doesn't know is how sick it made me to be around her, too. This is my mother, the real one. The woman we've seen for the last few months, the strong one, she was just a mask. This is the real lady. Come on. I can't stand to stay here one more second."

Ian nodded. "It's best we get out of here, but you should know we'll be watching."

They turned and left. Hector squeezed her hand again, making her ache before he finally let it go.

"I think you should start lunch," he said. "I'm hungry and I'm sure Dakota is as well."

She nodded. "Of course."

She turned and walked to the kitchen. This time, the voice in her head was utterly silent.

* * * *

Marcus felt his cell phone vibrate but he ignored it. It didn't matter. It was likely Brittany trying to explain why she'd turned away from him or his mother…

There was no explanation for what she'd done.

All around him Murphy's pub was alive with action and he felt so very stuck.

Stuck in Storm. Stuck in his family. Stuck in his life.

All around him people were moving through their day, having a life and building something. What was he going to do now?

He could still see his father standing there with a wicked smile on his face. He'd known he'd won.

"I don't know what to say to you, Marcus." Dillon sat down across from him, sliding a beer his way and then passing another to Ian.

"You don't have to say anything." He understood what Dillon had been doing.

"He should say he's sorry for not going through with his plan and killing the son of a bitch then and there," Logan added as he sat down. "When you've got a rabid dog, you don't bargain with it. You put it down for everyone's sake."

Sonya Murphy gasped and stared at her son. "Logan, how could you? What Dillon did was wrong and it could have cost him everything."

Dillon shrugged. "It still might."

Marcus looked at his friend. "Thank you for trying to look out for my mother."

Dillon's eyes were weary as he looked up. "I've been trying to look after her since we were kids. I don't know what else to do."

"You take a deep breath and try again," Sonya advised. She put a hand on Marcus's shoulder. "You've had a rough day, son. Let me get you something to eat. And you can stay with us for a while."

"Or with me," Ian offered.

He needed time to think. "I'll let you know what I decide. I'm not sure that I can eat a thing right now, but I appreciate the offer."

At least someone was looking out for him.

"I'll make something that will tempt you," Sonya declared. "All of you. You need to keep your energy up. There's nothing so bad it can't be fixed. You remember that."

He wasn't so sure about that. His parents seemed very broken indeed. His whole family, really. Everyone was talking about them all over again. The fight they'd had in town square would be talked about for months and months. Now they had the problem of Dakota spouting off. She would feed that gossip with some of her own if given the chance. She would tell everyone about what Dillon had done and how he'd tried to hurt her father. The gossip would flow straight to the Rushes. Every single rumor would be another mark against him in Marylee's book.

His cell buzzed again.

"Are you going to answer that?" Logan asked.

"It's Brittany." He took a drag off the beer. He could use a few of those, but he suspected Ian would cut him off at some point. It was comforting to know he wouldn't be allowed to trash his future the way he'd done during those first few months away from home. Knowing someone cared enough to fight for him gave him the strength to remain disciplined. "She wants to know how I'm doing. Well, she thinks she wants to know."

"So tell her," Ian encouraged.

"Tell her what? That my mom's back with my abusive father and I'm not welcome in her home until I kiss his ass? Should I tell her that? Should I tell her my sister is likely going to accuse the sheriff of abusing his position and throw us all into another scandal?"

Dillon cursed under his breath. "I'm sorry. I never thought he would come back. I really thought he was too much of a coward to come back. What happened? What's different now?"

Marcus shook his head. "No need to apologize. I could have told you that my father is a coward, but he's also stubborn. He went away and nursed his wounds and started plotting how to get back at you. He'll come at you hard, Dillon, and not in the way you expect."

"I'll have to be ready then. But I'm so sorry for the position it puts you in. If they hear about it, Sebastian and Marylee will use it to convince Brittany you're a bad bet."

"So fight them," Logan replied. "Talk to her. Give her a reason to stay together."

He was being naïve. Even if he convinced Brittany to

go against her family for him, there was another problem. One he wasn't sure he could ever solve. "So my family can tear her apart? My father is back and he'll stop at nothing to make sure I'm miserable. He'll go for the throat and find out every single weakness I have. And now I have a very big one."

"Brittany," Ian summed up.

"Women." Logan sat back with a sigh. "Our lives would be simpler without women."

"And completely devoid of any value," Dillon said. "Sometimes we just fall for the wrong ones. It seems to be our family curse."

"Joanne is afraid. She's scared," Ian said quietly. "I don't think she was choosing him as much as she was afraid of him."

"If she was scared, she's got plenty of people to turn to," Dillon replied with a sullen shake of his head. "She refuses to reach out. I have to think that maybe it's because she really loves that bastard and she's willing to do anything to stay with him."

"I don't know about that. But I do know he won't stop abusing her. Men like that never stop until someone takes care of them." Ian's eyes seemed a bit darker than before.

"Well, she sounded pretty damn strong when she told me to get out of her house." Dillon stared at his beer and Marcus figured he was probably going over that moment again in his head. "She looked at me like I was a piece of trash she wanted to sweep away."

Was his mother a lost cause? He didn't want to think so. He'd come to adore the strong woman she'd been when Hector was out of the picture. How could she go back to him? How could she not see that there were people who truly loved her and wanted to take care of her?

Everything had fallen apart so quickly.

He'd come home to help his mother move into the

future, but the minute she could, she'd chosen the past.

"I don't know what to do." Sometimes it made a man strong to admit his weakness. Ian had taught him that.

The man he wished had been his father reached out and put a hand on his. "We'll figure it out, son. We'll take it one day at a time."

Logan's hand came out, covering Ian's like they were a team about to head on the field. "I'm in for figuring out Marcus's life. It's gotta be more fun than figuring out my own."

For the first time since the scene at Marcus's house, Dillon's lips turned up in the approximation of a smile. He let his hand join theirs. "Sure. I'm in. Unless I have to fight to keep my job."

"I'll make sure you don't," Marcus offered. "One way or another, we'll make sure my sister keeps her mouth shut. My father won't talk. He won't want anyone to know he was beaten by you. And if it does come up, we deal with it together."

"I'll get us another round, brothers," Logan said, breaking the connection.

But he had a connection. This was what he hadn't had the first time around. Brothers.

He stared down at his phone. He couldn't call her back now. He had thinking to do.

At least he wouldn't do it alone.

* * * *

The story continues with Episode 5, Fire and Rain by R.K. Lilley.

About Lexi Blake

Lexi Blake lives in North Texas with her husband, three kids, and the laziest rescue dog in the world. She began writing at a young age, concentrating on plays and journalism. It wasn't until she started writing romance that she found success. She likes to find humor in the strangest places. Lexi believes in happy endings no matter how odd the couple, threesome or foursome may seem. She also writes contemporary Western ménage as Sophie Oak.

Connect with Lexi online:

Facebook: Lexi Blake
Twitter: https://twitter.com/authorlexiblake
Website: www.LexiBlake.net

Sign up for the Rising Storm/1001 Dark Nights Newsletter
and be entered to win an exclusive lightning bolt necklace
specially designed for Rising Storm by
Janet Cadsawan of Cadsawan.com.

Go to www.RisingStormBooks.com to subscribe.

As a bonus, all subscribers will receive a free
Rising Storm story
Storm Season: Ginny & Jacob – the Prequel
by Dee Davis

Rising Storm

Storm, Texas.

Where passion runs hot, desire runs deep, and secrets have the power to destroy…

Nestled among rolling hills and painted with vibrant wildflowers, the bucolic town of Storm, Texas, seems like nothing short of perfection.

But there are secrets beneath the facade. Dark secrets. Powerful secrets. The kind that can destroy lives and tear families apart. The kind that can cut through a town like a tempest, leaving jealousy and destruction in its wake, along with shattered hopes and broken dreams. All it takes is one little thing to shatter that polish.

Rising Storm is a series conceived by Julie Kenner and Dee Davis to read like an on-going drama. Set in a small Texas town, *Rising Storm* is full of scandal, deceit, romance, passion, and secrets. Lots of secrets.

Look for other Rising Storm Season 2 titles, now available! (And if you missed Season 1 and the midseason episodes, you can find those titles here!)

Rising Storm, Season Two

Against the Wind by Rebecca Zanetti
As Tate Johnson works to find a balance between his

ambitions for political office and the fallout of his brother's betrayal, Zeke is confronted with his brother Chase's return home. And while Bryce and Tara Daniels try to hold onto their marriage, Kristin continues to entice Travis into breaking his vows...

Storm Warning by Larissa Ione

As Joanne Alvarez settles into life without Hector, her children still struggle with the fallout. Marcus confronts the differences between him and Brittany, while Dakota tries to find a new equilibrium. Meanwhile, the Johnson's grapple with war between two sets of brothers, and Ian Briggs rides into town...

Brave the Storm by Lisa Mondello

As Senator Rush's poll numbers free fall, Marylee tries to drive a wedge between Brittany and Marcus. Across town, Anna Mae and Chase dance toward reconciliation. Ginny longs for Logan, while he fights against Sebastian's maneuvering. And Hector, newly freed from prison, heads back to Storm...

Lightning Strikes by Lexi Blake

As Ian Briggs begins to fall for Marisol, Joanne and Dillon also grow closer. Joanne's new confidence spreads to Dakota but Hector's return upends everything. A public confrontation between Marcus and Hector endangers his relationship with Brittany, and Dakota reverts to form. Meanwhile, the Senator threatens Ginny and the baby...

Fire and Rain by R.K. Lilley

As Celeste Salt continues to unravel in the wake of Jacob's death, Travis grows closer with Kristin. Lacey realizes the error of her ways but is afraid it's too late for reconciliation with her friends. Marcus and Brittany struggle with the continued fallout of Hector's return, while Chase and Anna Mae face some hard truths about their past…

Quiet Storm by Julie Kenner

As Mallory Alvarez and Luis Moreno grow closer, Lacey longs for forgiveness. Brittany and Marcus have a true meeting of hearts. Meanwhile, Jeffry grapples with his father's failures and finds solace in unexpected arms. When things take a dangerous turn, Jeffry's mother and sister, as well as his friends, unite behind him as the Senator threatens his son…

Blinding Rain by Elisabeth Naughton

As Tate Johnson struggles to deal with his brother's relationship with Hannah, hope asserts itself in an unexpected way. With the return of Delia Burke, Logan's old flame, Brittany and Marcus see an opportunity to help their friend. But when the evening takes an unexpected turn, Brittany finds herself doing the last thing she expected—coming face to face with Ginny…

Blue Skies by Dee Davis

As Celeste Salt struggles to pull herself and her family together, Dillon is called to the scene of a domestic dispute where Dakota is forced to face the truth about her father. While the Johnson's celebrate a big announcement, Ginny is rushed to the hospital where her baby's father is finally revealed…

Rising Storm, Midseason

After the Storm by Lexi Blake

In the wake of Dakota's revelations, the whole town is reeling. Ginny Moreno has lost everything. Logan Murphy is devastated by her lies. Brittany Rush sees her family in a horrifying new light. And nothing will ever be the same...

Distant Thunder by Larissa Ione
As Sebastian and Marylee plot to cover up Sebastian's sexual escapade, Ginny and Dakota continue to reel from the fallout of Dakota's announcement. But it is the Rush family that's left to pick up the pieces as Payton, Brittany and Jeffry each cope with Sebastian's betrayal in their own way...

Rising Storm, Season One

Tempest Rising by Julie Kenner
Ginny Moreno didn't mean to do it, but when she came home to Storm, she brought the tempest with her. And now everyone will be caught in its fury...

White Lightning by Lexi Blake
As the citizens of Storm, Texas, sway in the wake of the death of one of their own, Daddy's girl Dakota Alvarez also reels from an unexpected family crisis... and finds consolation in a most unexpected place.

Crosswinds by Elisabeth Naughton
Lacey Salt's world shattered with the death of her brother, and now the usually sweet-tempered girl is determined to take back some control—even if that means sabotaging her best friend, Mallory, and Mallory's new boyfriend, Luis.

Dance in the Wind by Jennifer Probst
During his time in Afghanistan, Logan Murphy has endured the unthinkable, but reentering civilian life in Storm is harder than he imagined. But when he is

reacquainted with Ginny Moreno, a woman who has survived terrors of her own, he feels the first stirrings of hope.

Calm Before the Storm by Larissa Ione
Marcus Alvarez fled Storm when his father's drinking drove him over the edge. With his mother and sisters in crisis, Marcus is forced to return to the town he thought he'd left behind. But it is his attraction to a very grown up Brittany Rush that just might be enough to guarantee that he stays.

Take the Storm by Rebecca Zanetti
Marisol Moreno has spent her youth taking care of her younger siblings. Now, with her sister, Ginny, in crisis, and her brother in the throes of his first real relationship, she doesn't have time for anything else. Especially not the overtures of the incredibly compelling Patrick Murphy.

Weather the Storm by Lisa Mondello
Bryce Douglas faces a crisis of faith when his idyllic view of his family is challenged with his son's diagnosis of autism. Instead of accepting his wife and her tight-knit family's comfort, he pushes them away, fears from his past threatening to undo the happiness he's found in his present.

Thunder Rolls by Dee Davis
In the season finale …

As Hannah Grossman grapples with the very real possibility that she is dating one Johnson brother while secretly in love with another, the entire town prepares for Founders Day. The building tempest threatens not just Hannah's relationship with Tucker and Tate, but everyone in Storm as dire revelations threaten to tear the town apart.

Fire and Rain

Rising Storm, Season 2, Episode 5
By R.K. Lilley
Now Available

Secrets, Sex and Scandals ...

Welcome to Storm, Texas, where passion runs hot, desire runs deep, and secrets have the power to destroy... Get ready. The storm is coming.

As Celeste Salt continues to unravel in the wake of Jacob's death, Travis grows closer with Kristin. Lacey realizes the error of her ways but is afraid it's too late for reconciliation with her friends. Marcus and Brittany struggle with the continued fallout of Hector's return, while Chase and Anna Mae face some hard truths about their past...

* * * *

Travis Salt studied his wife with a carefully gentle detachment.

She was a mess. She'd been unraveling for a while, it was clear. A slow and steady decline since Jacob's death, but things seemed to have taken a definite turn for the worse.

"Can I get you anything?" His voice rang out pleasantly, and he hoped it showed the amount of concern she deserved, whether he felt it or not.

They were in their bedroom, it was past noon, and Celeste clearly had no intention of crawling out of bed, let alone showering or getting dressed.

His wife's red-rimmed eyes swung to him, but she looked right through him. There he was, sacrificing his own wants and desires to please her, and she barely saw him.

When had this happened? And who was to blame? Which one of them had checked out of their marriage to the point that they took so little notice of each other anymore?

He didn't let his mind linger on that question, because it didn't really matter. The fact was that he didn't know what to do with her, and he'd been trying his best.

Well, the best that could be expected from a man with one foot out the door.

He frowned to himself. It was his day off from the pharmacy, but he'd already come up with at least a dozen excuses why he had to go into work.

He wondered if he even needed to voice one aloud. He doubted Celeste would even notice in her current state.

Then again, he supposed it could be worse. She could be passed out drunk at the cemetery again.

"Perhaps some tea?" He eyed the full glass of water by the bed. He'd placed it there the night before. "A fresh glass of water?"

She didn't respond but her eyes shut suddenly, fresh tears seeping out.

In spite of everything, he felt something in him twist in pain, and not just for their lost son.

Did he still love Celeste? Yes, he reflected. Some part of his heart would always remain soft for this gentle, loving woman who had put her all into being a mother to his children. He wanted her to do well, to get better, and to be there for their daughters. To stand on her own two feet without him.

He wanted her to have that strength, yes. But mostly he had to admit that he wanted her to stand alone so that he would be free to leave.

Because while some part of him might still love his wife, his heart belonged elsewhere. He was, above all, a man. A selfish one. And he'd become completely wrapped up in someone that made him feel passionate, alive again, and younger than his years.

Kristin.

1001 Dark Nights

Welcome to 1001 Dark Nights… a collection of novellas that are breathtakingly sexy and magically romantic. Some are paranormal, some are erotic. Each and every one is compelling and page turning.

Inspired by the exotic tales of The Arabian Nights, 1001 Dark Nights features *New York Times* and *USA Today* bestselling authors.

In the original, Scheherazade desperately attempts to entertain her husband, the King of Persia, with nightly stories so that he will postpone her execution.

In our version, month after month, each of our fabulous authors puts a unique spin on the premise and creates a tale that a new Scheherazade tells long into the dark, dark night.

For more information about 1001 Dark Nights, visit www.1001DarkNights.com.

On behalf of Rising Storm,

Liz Berry, M.J. Rose, Julie Kenner & Dee Davis would like
to thank ~

Steve Berry
Doug Scofield
Melissa Rheinlander
Kim Guidroz
Jillian Stein
InkSlinger PR
Asha Hossain
Chris Graham
Pamela Jamison
Fedora Chen
Jessica Johns
Dylan Stockton
Richard Blake
The Dinner Party Show
and Simon Lipskar

CPSIA information can be obtained
at www.ICGtesting.com
Printed in the USA
LVHW02s2012110518
576873LV00001B/56/P